A Candlelight Ecstasy Romance®

**"I'VE HAD IT WITH YOUR LIES. BEFORE TONIGHT IS OVER, I WANT TO KNOW EVERYTHING ABOUT YOU."**

"Isn't this moral indignation a little misplaced?" Raine snapped. "I'm the one who should be mad at you for trying to seduce me so that I'd buy your lithograph."

Ari's dark eyes flashed dangerously, and suddenly she was down on the sand, her arms pinned over her head. "Everything I said was true, Raine. We could have so much together. Why do you keep lying to me?"

"What difference does it make?" she answered, struggling to free her hands. "All you need to know about me is that my check is good."

## CANDLELIGHT ECSTASY ROMANCES®

322  SKY GYPSY, *Natalie Stone*
323  TWO SEPARATE LIVES, *Tate McKenna*
324  ENCORE OF DESIRE, *Jan Stuart*
325  WHERE LOVE MAY LEAD, *Eleanor Woods*
326  MORE PRECIOUS THAN GOLD, *Cindy Victor*
327  A DISTANT SUMMER, *Karen Whittenburg*
328  FRIENDS AND LOVERS, *Emily Elliott*
329  LOVING PERSUASION, *Emma Bennett*
330  A GLIMPSE OF PARADISE, *Cathie Linz*
331  WITH EACH CARESS, *Anne Silverlock*
332  JUST A KISS AWAY, *JoAnna Brandon*
333  WHEN MIDNIGHT COMES, *Edith Delatush*
334  MORE THAN A DREAM, *Lynn Patrick*
335  HOLD CLOSE THE MEMORY, *Heather Graham*
336  A VISION OF LOVE, *Melanie Catley*
337  DIAMOND IN THE ROUGH, *Joan Grove*
338  LOVING LESSONS, *Barbara Andrews*
339  ROMANTIC ROULETTE, *Jackie Black*
340  HIDEAWAY, *Carol Norris*
341  NO RESERVATIONS, *Molly Katz*
342  WANTED: MAN TO LOVE, *Evelyn Coate*
343  SURPRISE PACKAGE, *Emily Elliott*
344  TILL MORNING'S LIGHT, *Sheila Paulos*
345  A WHOLE LOT OF WOMAN, *Anna Hudson*

# STEAL A RAINBOW

*Sue Gross*

*A CANDLELIGHT ECSTASY ROMANCE*®

Published by
Dell Publishing Co., Inc.
1 Dag Hammarskjold Plaza
New York, New York 10017

Copyright © 1985 by Sue Gross

All rights reserved. No part of this book may be reproduced
or transmitted in any form or by any means, electronic or
mechanical, including photocopying, recording or by any
information storage and retrieval system, without the written
permission of the Publisher, except where permitted by law.

Dell ® TM 681510, Dell Publishing Co., Inc.

Candlelight Ecstasy Romance®, 1,203,540, is a registered
trademark of Dell Publishing Co., Inc., New York, New York.

ISBN: 0-440-18326-X

Printed in the United States of America

First printing—July 1985

To Our Readers:

We have been delighted with your enthusiastic response to Candlelight Ecstasy Romances®, and we thank you for the interest you have shown in this exciting series.

In the upcoming months we will continue to present the distinctive sensuous love stories you have come to expect only from Ecstasy. We look forward to bringing you many more books from your favorite authors and also the very finest work from new authors of contemporary romantic fiction.

As always, we are striving to present the unique, absorbing love stories that you enjoy most—books that are more than ordinary romance.
la1l]Your suggestions and comments are always welcome. Please write to us at the address below.

    Sincerely,

    The Editors
    Candlelight Romances
    1 Dag Hammarskjold Plaza
    New York, New York 10017

# CHAPTER ONE

"Let's face it, the rich are different," Raine declared with a laugh as she and her sister walked up famed Rodeo Drive in Beverly Hills. "I think I know how the bedraggled crusaders felt when they caught their first glimpse of Byzantium."

"Come on, Raine, Byzantium was never this lush. There's enough polished brass and marble on this one street to sink a battleship. I've just counted six Mercedes and two Rolls-Royces in the past thirty seconds. Whoops, three."

A white-gloved, liveried doorman rushed past them to open the door of a silver Rolls limousine. A tanned middle-aged woman in a suede pantsuit stepped daintily out of the car and swept into a boutique.

"Let's see what she buys," suggested Janet in a conspiratorial whisper.

Feeling like spies, the two sisters tried to look blasé as they meandered casually after the woman into the shoe department and watched wide-eyed as she bought a pair of orange sandals for three hundred and ninety-seven dollars.

"There were only two little teeny straps on those things," said Janet, aghast, as they walked out of the store.

"But they matched her hair perfectly."

"Big deal," Janet scoffed. "I saw the exact same

sandal at the Glendale Galleria for fifteen ninety-five. That dummy in the false eyelashes just got taken to the cleaners and she didn't even know it."

"Or didn't care," Raine corrected as she brushed a wisp of auburn hair off her forehead. "If she can afford to have the chauffeur double-park the Rolls—"

"Wasting gas," Janet interjected.

"—then she can probably afford a little rip-off now and then."

Janet winced. "Three hundred and ninety-seven dollars for a pair of sandals? That's not a rip-off, it's grand larceny!"

"Wouldn't it be nice to be able to spend that kind of money without batting an eyelash," said Raine whimsically.

"Her eyelashes alone probably cost her ninety-seven dollars," grumbled Janet.

"But it sort of puts things in perspective. I'm glad you suggested we come out here slumming tonight to see how the other half lives."

"If only they didn't live so stupidly. It bothers me to see anyone get taken like that."

"Relax, Janet, we're off duty tonight. *Buyer Beware* only pays us to dig up stories about the poor and disadvantaged consumer."

"I know, but what right do we have to discriminate against the rich? We publish supermarket surveys each week to save shoppers five and ten dollars on groceries and then stand by and do nothing when an unsuspecting minority, namely the rich, is getting fleeced for hundreds of thousands."

Raine had to laugh. Her sister regarded her work with the fervor of a religious crusader. "Janet, who is going to shed a tear over the plight of a woman who can fork over someone's weekly salary for a pair of sandals?"

"I think it would make our readers feel better to know they're not the only ones getting taken in the marketplace," argued Janet. "In fact I think it's worth a whole series. Let's talk to McCracken about it Monday. We could call it 'Rip-offs of the Rich.' "

Raine glanced around at the elegant stores, Gucci, Giorgio, Yves Saint Laurent, Hermès. "On second thought, doing research out here in the wild hills of Beverly would be a welcome change from those slimy auto-body shops I had to frequent for my last story."

"You know that woman with the sandals had a cute hairdo, Raine. I'd love to see something like that on you. You're so careless about your appearance, and since you've decided to grow your hair out long, it always seems to be falling in your face. Oh, and, hon, you need lipstick. You've eaten yours all off."

Raine stiffened even as she automatically brushed her hair off her face and dug into her purse for lipstick. She adored her older sister and knew she should be grateful for these constant critiques, but more and more lately they were simply irksome.

They turned the corner at Brighton Way, and as they passed an art gallery, Raine looked in the window and grabbed Janet's arm. "Would you look at that!"

"What?"

"That painting. It's beautiful!"

Janet squinted. "If you say so. I don't know beans about art."

The huge abstract painting created the illusion that one was looking inside a giant crystal infused with sunlight. Planes of varying widths seemed to act as prisms, refracting shimmering rainbows in every direction.

Raine's chest constricted and tears filled her eyes. She'd been to dozens of art museums, but nothing had never affected her at such a deep emotional level.

Drawn into the gallery, she walked slowly around the room, studying each painting and lithograph, one more captivating than the next. It was almost as though the light in them was changing, dancing playfully with her movements, translucent one minute, reflecting her auburn hair and green dress the next.

Sitting at the back of the gallery, Ari Lekas had been observing the two young women. The resemblance between them was so strong that they had to be sisters, but his artist's eye caught the differences. The animated one with the short, stylish auburn hair was the prettiest. She had the kind of dynamic fire that had always attracted him in a woman. He watched her move with purpose from piece to piece, not looking at them, but searching in vain for price tags.

With more makeup the other one might have been as striking as her sister. There was something quiet and wide-eyed about her. If she had not been looking at his paintings with such an awestruck expression, he probably wouldn't have noticed her at all. But tonight that was enough to win his heart.

It had been a bad night for an artist's ego. The gallery had been filled with tourists who asked prices, laughed about them, then trekked into the next store to repeat the performance. The worst had been the loud-mouthed conventioneers who thought that because he spoke with an accent he was dumb enough to believe they were wealthy Texas oil men on a buying spree. They had so drained him of his limited capacity to be civil that he had decided to sit out the rest of the evening at the far end of the gallery, speaking to no one.

Until these two young women walked in. Ari had spent enough time among wealthy art collectors to know that they were expensively dressed in the latest fashions, yet aside from an exotic brass necklace on the one with the short hair, neither was wearing any jewelry. But then nobody with any brains wore expensive jewelry on the street, even if that street was Rodeo Drive.

He cut off his own train of thought. What irony. If it weren't so tragic, he'd laugh at himself for this calculated pocketbook analysis of each potential customer. Had the barracuda pond they called Beverly Hills already transformed him into a wily, cynical businessman? His father would call it just revenge for all the unkind things he'd said about the business world when he was growing up. Art had been all that mattered to him, and now here he was in the most expensive marketplace in the world, hawking his wares as if they were cheap souvenirs.

The whimsical one was staring enrapt at his favorite lithograph. He was enjoying the interaction between the woman and his work, how the unusual shade of her hair played off against the colors in it. He found himself thinking how that thick hair, unfettered, would fall heavily onto her slender shoulders like a flaming waterfall. There was a sultry quality about her a man wouldn't notice at first glance that lingered just under the surface of her pale skin. It was probably something she wasn't even aware of, and it made him think of the first time he had looked into a prism and begun dreaming of the treasures it could yield if he tried to paint what he saw.

An elderly couple walked in. They were conservatively dressed, with a look of culture and intelligence about them, the kind of people experience had taught him were potential customers, but he ignored them. The green-eyed girl had moved around to the edge of the lithograph. It was an angle few people ever noticed, but from there one could see a face nearly hidden in the rainbows. Her eyes grew wider, her lips parted slightly, and she caught her breath. A man would sell his soul to have a woman look at him like that. Breaking his vow to remain aloof the rest of the evening, he stood up, stretched his long legs, and walked toward her.

As he approached, her sister said, "You really like that, Raine, don't you?"

"It's splendid."

Raine watched with amusement as Janet took another appraising look at the lithograph, trying to make out what her sister saw in it, then returned to her own measure for all things. "I wonder how much it costs."

"Ten thousand dollars," Ari answered, hoping he didn't sound as amazed as he always was when he quoted his own exorbitant prices. But if that's what Nicole, damn her, had gotten for his work, why shouldn't he? After all, he was the one who had worked the long hours to produce it.

Raine turned and looked up into deep-set eyes so black they seemed like onyx. He was tall and lean, but with powerful shoulders. A tailored white linen suit set off a deep tan, and though the accent was vaguely Mediterranean, the blond hair was an intriguing contrast to it. To Raine's amazement the man affected her like the artwork. A molten sheet of light swept up from her toes and wrapped her in its folds.

Janet, however, remained unmoved. "Only ten thousand? What the heck, Rainey, as long as you like it, buy it. It would look marvelous in the Malibu house."

Raine had to stifle a laugh. She couldn't even afford the frame. When they were children, she and Janet had played these make-believe games with people. Even though it was in good fun, lying of any kind always made Raine uneasy, and she was the one who usually ended up by blurting out the truth before it went too far. Since they had become consumer reporters, however, the playacting had become a necessary tool. By posing as an unsuspecting "dizzy dame" with a smashed bumper, she had just made a revealing tour of auto-body shops collecting repair estimates that ran from two hundred to two thousand dollars. She'd even won a prestigious journalism award for an exposé on nursing home abuse by getting a job in one and taking shocking pictures with a hidden camera.

But tonight, standing between the glittering paintings and this magnetic man, she found it hard to wear a mask. It was as though she had walked into a magic kingdom where one was immediately stripped of all pretense and subterfuge.

"In fact," said Janet, "if you like it so much, buy two. We'll ship one back to Aunt Beatrice in Lake Forest."

Raine couldn't help but muse that their Aunt Bea thought the golden age of modern art ended with Norman Rockwell. "It seems impossible there'd be two of these," she murmured. She couldn't pull her gaze away from the onyx eyes that were studying her with unnerving intensity. Though she forced herself to look at the lithograph, the dancing lights in it only heightened the fiery turbulence flowing through her veins.

"There are a total of six of them, signed and numbered," he said.

"Where are the other five?" asked Janet.

"One is in the permanent collection of the Museum of Modern Art in New York, one in the Museum of Contemporary Art in Dallas, two are in private collections, and I have one at home in my studio."

"I still think it would look terrific in the Malibu house," said Janet. "Let's surprise Mom and get it for her."

"One of the editions is, in fact, in a private home in

Malibu," said Ari. "It's overlooking the sea. I have a picture. Let me show you."

Raine watched him as he walked across the gallery. There was an air of drama about him that made it difficult to draw her eyes away. Rainbows from his paintings seemed to reflect off his white suit, and she wondered fancifully if he wouldn't attract rainbows anywhere he went.

In the photograph he showed them the lithograph was displayed against a backdrop of rugged California coastline. It was a strange effect, but it almost seemed to become a part of the landscape. "Here's a photograph taken of one of my paintings in the desert at sunset."

She studied the photos, carefully comparing them to the work in the studio. "It's as though it gathered the scenery into itself and then reinterpreted it on its own terms," she said with wonder. "In this room the painting appears to be obsessed with manufacturing rainbows, yet in the desert it seems to be clothing itself in rays from the setting sun. I've never seen anything like it before. Even the shapes in them are elusive and seem to change as you move to one side or another. A moment ago I even thought I saw a face in this one, but now it's gone. This art is like a wild fantasy, all magic mirrors and crystal balls and windows and light."

Ari gazed at her in utter amazement. "Do you know that you are the first person ever to walk into this gallery who understood what I was trying to do?"

"You're the artist?"

She might have known by the way he affected her. It seemed only fitting that a man who could create such enchantment would himself be something of a spellbinder.

"Working here in the gallery, I've found they react differently to each person, as though they could take on their colorations and personalities. As I was watching you there was something unique and beautiful happening I've never seen before."

"Amazing," said Janet. Raine could tell by her sister's tone that she wasn't taken in. A natural cynic, Janet had honed her skepticism with a lifelong commitment to consumerism. She heard only the slick sales pitch in his words. And though Raine fought it, her glittering enchantment with the painter was now also tarnished. Both she and Janet had worked in their parents' appliance store and knew a good sales pitch when they heard one. Flattery, their mother had hammered into their heads as soon as they could reach their heads up behind a counter, was one of the quickest ways to a sale, and women were the most susceptible to that technique.

But whatever she thought of the technique, Raine was still enchanted by the work itself. Walking slowly around the room, she drank it in. "I would love to have one of these," she whispered. "They are the most beautiful . . . most exciting works of art I've ever seen in my entire life."

"Then you should have one," he said.

Did he really think she could afford a ten-thousand-dollar lithograph? If he knew anything about clothes, he would assume she could. Two years ago she and Janet had done a series on the downtown bargain stores where sample designer clothes could be purchased for next to nothing. She was wearing a thirty-dollar dress that probably retailed for two hundred dollars.

"Ten thousand dollars is a little steep for something you hang on the wall," said Janet practically. "It's not as if you were buying a car—something that will at least take you to the hairdresser and back."

Raine saw a muscle tighten in his face, and his eyes

flashed momentarily. His voice was harder when he spoke, as though he were trying to keep his animosity in check.

"Not if you look at it as an investment," he said mechanically. "With only six of them in existence, when this one is sold, the last one will go up to twenty thousand dollars."

Janet's mouth dropped. "You'd double back your investment?"

"Every time one is sold, the next doubles in price," he explained. "And when they are all gone, any edition is worth the final price, sometimes more."

"Is there a way to write it off on your income tax?" Having just completed an article on the subject, Janet was up on tax loopholes.

"If you can use it for your business. What sort of business are you in?" he asked Raine.

"Oh, she doesn't work at all."

"Janet . . ."

"Well, why work if you don't have to?" Janet said flippantly.

"Actually, I'm a writer," said Raine in spite of Janet's warning look. He had to know he was being put on, and if he didn't, she wasn't interested in stringing him along any farther. She tried to read the man's eyes, but they were dark and impenetrable, unlike his paintings, which were flowing with light. For a brief moment she thought she saw a trace of sadness in their depths, but it quickly disappeared.

"Raine dabbles at writing," Janet explained quickly. "Kind of obscure but lovely romantic poetry. Mother had it published for her a few years ago."

"Ah, a poet! That explains your reaction to my work and why you can put it so beautifully into words."

Janet wasn't lying about her poetry. For years her

sister had been trying to persuade her to look for a publisher, but Raine had always felt her poetry was too personal. She was embarrassed to show it to a stranger. As a birthday present a few years ago Janet had used the printing facilities at *Buyer Beware* to make fifty hand-bound pamphlets of Raine's best poems so she could see "how good they look in print." But as tickled as she was by Janet's gesture, Raine was still too timid to look for a legitimate publisher.

"You would have to speak to your accountant," he said, "but I don't see why you couldn't claim that you needed the litho for poetic inspiration." He handed her his card. "My name is Ari Lekas. If you would like to discuss it, I would be happy to meet with you again."

"Thank you, but—"

"I'm sure she'll call you," said Janet quickly. "By the way, my name is Janet Walken, and this is my sister, Raine."

"Like the rain from the sky?" he asked.

She flushed. "Yes, but with an *e* on the end."

"It is great pleasure to meet you both," he said. "And I hope I'll be hearing from you."

"Oh, I don't think—"

"Raine, you know you want it," prodded Janet.

"Perhaps you would like to talk it over with your mother," Ari suggested.

"Why not, Raine? Mom's beach house would be a perfect setting for it, all modern style with lots of wood and picture windows."

Raine was amused to hear Janet describe their publisher's home in Malibu.

"You have my card," said Ari. "Call me next week."

He extended his hand to Raine, and when she took

it, a rainbow seemed to shimmer out of the painting and to spiral through her body.

Her feet barely skimmed the floor as she floated out of the gallery. "I feel as though I've just had a close encounter of the third kind."

"We've got to do this story," said Janet enthusiastically. "That picture was nice, but no way was it worth any ten thousand dollars."

"Janet, you don't price a Michelangelo sculpture by weighing the marble," she responded defensively. "We're not dealing with shoes or car bumpers. That was a magnificent work of art!"

"And a magnificent hunk of masculinity," Janet added slyly, "with those black eyes and blond hair. I know how you get carried away by those artsy types. I bet if you went down to the Design Center or some of the lower-priced art galleries on Melrose, you could find the same stuff for half or even a quarter of that. He's got those prices all jacked up because he's on Rodeo Drive. It's just like those fifteen ninety-five sandals selling for three hundred and ninety-seven dollars."

It was futile to argue with Janet when she was on a soapbox. Raine had long ago accepted the fact that her sister was passionately committed to righting all the wrongs done to shoppers of the world.

When they'd both arrived in California, Janet, who had been a consumer activist in Chicago, had found a job right away at *Buyer Beware*. All Raine had ever wanted to be was a poet, but that was about as practical as wanting to be a gazelle. Wanting to work creatively in some way with words, she had majored in journalism. But after two months in Los Angeles she'd had no luck in finding a job even remotely related to writing. So when a reporter's job opened up at *Buyer Beware,* Janet urged her to take it. "I know you're not crazy about doing exposés on things like generic drug prices," she told Raine, "but let's face it, poetry isn't going to pay the electric bill."

The trouble was poetry needed inspiration, and there were few muses hanging around auto-body shops and discount furniture stores. It had been over a year since Raine had felt the urge to write a poem.

Janet was convinced that her sister's recent lack of productivity was proof that her interest in poetry was waning. "Now aren't you glad I talked you into taking journalism instead of creative writing? You may not have a practical bone in your body, but at least you have me to set you straight when you go wandering up in the clouds."

Janet had been four years old when the new baby was brought home, and she had been told that her new sister would be her special responsibility. Responsibility was not something Janet took lightly, even at four, and since then, looking out for Raine had become something of a secondary career.

It was only lately that Raine, at twenty-two, had begun to assert herself. When Janet hadn't liked the classical guitarist Raine was dating, the tension grew to such a point that Raine, in an uncharacteristic fit of rebellion, had moved into her own apartment. When the guitarist dropped her, Janet begged her to move back in.

It had been tempting to return to that security, but Raine realized she liked being on her own. It meant being able to drop clothes on the floor with nobody nagging at you to pick them up, or being able to munch a chocolate bar without being reminded how it would affect your skin or waistline. She only wished Janet could understand. "Constantly having to look out for someone doesn't leave you much freedom either," she had tried to explain. Maybe her life wasn't very well organized and there were moments of loneliness, but the heady sense of independence was well worth it.

Raine tried to sleep when she got back to her apartment that night, but only tossed and turned in bed, twisting the sheets under her. When she closed her eyes, she saw the glittering paintings, like crystal shrines to some space-age gods, and the golden-haired artist in his white suit of rainbows as their chosen prophet. Turning on her lamp, she took out her note book and began to write . . .

> Steal the rainbows
> from the skies,
> The sea and desert winds,
> And hide them behind
> Onyx eyes;
> Then cut them
> into mystic crystals
> Glowing shrines
> that beckon maidens in the night.

Reading it over, she felt a quiet contentment. She'd nearly forgotten how good it felt to blend words and emotions, sounds and images—a process, she mused, not unlike creating a painting.

Suddenly she was possessed by an aching desire to share the poem with him. She turned his business card over in her hand. If she wanted to see him again, she'd have to make the call. He didn't have her number.

But would he want to see her if he knew she was barely squeaking by with car payments on a four-year-old Mustang? She reread her poem. It was worth a chance. She'd call him up Monday morning, tell him the truth about herself, and see what happened.

Closing her eyes, she thought about the dark-eyed prophet in white standing amid his crystal icons, and feeling whimsical and poetic, she slipped his business card under her pillow for luck, and went to sleep.

## CHAPTER TWO

*Buyer Beware* features editor Bart McCracken took a sip of hot coffee and frowned. Raine had come to recognize that frown as a sign of approval and dreaded what he was about to say. "It's not a bad idea. Not bad at all."

"Come on, McCracken," Raine said, shifting uncomfortably in the conference room chair. "Who cares how the rich waste their money?"

He mashed a cigarette into an already overflowing ashtray. "There's a kind of vicarious, slightly malicious thrill in it. And I'm crazy about the art angle. It's not just the wealthy who are investing in art nowadays. I had a friend who bought a Picasso sketch for five thousand dollars—a small little thing all signed and framed. Turned out it was a print, so perfectly done that you couldn't tell the difference, but it was worth maybe twenty dollars tops."

He scribbled some notes on his clipboard. "Let's start with the art gallery scams, then we'll move into other areas. Janet, you look at the investment angle, tax write-offs, that sort of thing, and, Raine"—he pointed his ballpoint pen at her—"you continue to pretend you're a serious buyer. Meet with this painter and see what his sales pitch is, then check with other galleries to get a price comparison."

"But we're dealing with original art," she protested.

"You can't put a set value on it as if it were a . . . a typewriter or something."

"Everything has a price tag on it. Even the 'Mona Lisa.' "

"That's hanging in a permanent collection in the Louvre," she argued.

"If somebody stole it, you'd bet they'd get a pretty penny for it."

As they walked out of the conference room, Janet took her aside. "This is no time to get maudlin, Raine. Your painter is gorgeous and he might be a talented artist, but he told you that litho was worth ten thousand dollars, and he tried to make you think that it's going to double in value after you buy it. That's as bad as the developers who used to sell parcels of desert land, telling people their property would double in value as soon as the airport went in. Twenty years later, still no airport and they're all stuck with acres of sand."

"How do you know he's lying?" asked Raine. "The price of his work might just be escalating that fast."

"You really believe that?"

"All right, I don't. But I also don't feel right about this."

Her sister leaned up against a wall and sighed. "I know exactly what you're feeling. I saw that look on your face when you started going with that guitarist. It's called worship. If Ari Lekas was a used-car salesman, you wouldn't hesitate a minute to go after this story."

"That has nothing to do with it."

"I know you, Raine. You'd like to believe people in the arts are better than ordinary mortals. Just because your guitarist could play a Bach fugue didn't make him less of a cad when he started standing you up. This Lekas guy may be a talented artist, but he's also a hard-nosed business man, and he was flattering you shamelessly to make that sale. You're such a dreamy romantic, and I love that in you, but if I didn't set you straight, you'd fall right down into the same pit all over again."

Raine knew her sister was right, and she was lucky to have someone who cared enough about her to wash the stars out of her eyes when she got carried away. Even so, she was uncomfortable dialing the gallery number. This was not the way she had envisioned beginning this relationship.

"Ari Lekas Gallery," he answered.

"Mr. Lekas, it's Raine Walken, you remember I was in the other night with my sister."

"I remember very well." His voice was deep and caressing, even over the phone. "In fact I was just thinking about you, hoping you'd call. When can I take you to lunch?"

"Today, if you'd like." She hoped he couldn't detect the tremor in her voice.

"Can you meet me here at the gallery at noon?"

"Yes, certainly."

"Good. And bring your poetry. I'm anxious to read it."

Her hand trembled as she replaced the receiver. This was going to be more difficult than car bumpers.

She was hoping Beverly Hills would lose some of its flash and glitter in the daylight, but this was not like Las Vegas, a city that turned into a tacky pumpkin at sunup. In the bright, unyielding light of high noon the Yellow Brick Road called Rodeo Drive managed to look even more like the mythical Emerald City than it did at nighttime.

Since she was early and didn't want to appear overeager to see him, she meandered into Yves Saint Laurent and tried to distract herself by wrapping hundred-dollar silk scarves around her neck. It didn't work. "Not quite what I was looking for," she told the saleslady and escaped back onto the street.

She had rushed home to change from the jeans she usually wore to work into something more suitable and had settled on a loose-fitting yellow linen pantsuit with a leather and brass belt that wrapped around her three times, showing off her slender waist. It had the kind of high style she thought appropriate for a Beverly Hills lunch. How much easier it had been to dress for auto-body shops.

Her heart began thumping uncontrollably the moment she saw the gallery, and she had to will her knees to remain steady as she walked in.

A thin young man in a suit and tie came toward her. "Are you Miss Walken?"

She nodded.

"Mr. Lekas will be with you in a minute. Would you care to sit down while you wait?"

"Uh, no thanks. I'll just wander around."

The paintings seemed slightly toned down without all the high wattage from the nighttime spotlights focused on them, but the natural light streaming in from the windows gave them a slightly different, still enchanting look. This time she tried to view them more objectively to see what made them so exciting, though that was like trying to dissect a sunset inch by inch. They were all fanciful works that boldly defied light and space. And if you really looked closely, you could see faces and figures in what seemed to be some highly erotic poses, though it was far too subtle to interest the centerfold folks at *Penthouse* and vague enough to make you think the illusions were yours, not the artist's intentions. She felt a little like a gypsy fortune-teller gazing into a crystal ball and seeing the kaleidoscopic fantasies of sculpted light beams.

She was so engrossed in the work that she did not hear Ari come up behind her. "Sorry to keep you waiting," he said. "I was on a long-distance call."

"I was enjoying myself," she said brightly as she turned, then steadied herself at the sight of him. If he had looked like a plantation owner the other night in his white linen suit, today he looked every inch the successful Beverly Hills businessman. There was an aristocratic elegance about his camel slacks, dark blue sports jacket, light blue pin-striped shirt, and deep maroon knit tie. His eyes seemed darker than she remembered and much more compelling.

"It's good to see you again," he said, extending his hand.

She swallowed hard. The moment she took his hand, all the rainbows wrapped themselves around her chest, constricting her vocal cords. "It's . . . good to see you, too." Get ahold of yourself, Raine, she warned herself, but even trying to think of him as a used-car salesman didn't work.

"How do you feel about French food?" he asked pleasantly.

"I'm crazy about it."

"Good. I know a place you'll like."

As he placed his large hand at the small of her back to lead her out of the gallery, she felt another shimmer of prismatic light shoot through her. It was good he was driving. Since she was having trouble putting one foot solidly in front of the other, she doubted her ability to put a car in gear.

They walked down the street to a parking lot, and she tried not to gape as he opened the door to a sleek black Italian sports car. "It's a beauty of a car," she murmured as he started the engine.

"It's a pain in the neck. In the shop more than it's out, and parts cost a king's ransom—if and when they're available. It was a crazy idea to buy it."

"Why did you?"

Ari sighed and smiled. "When I was a child growing up on the island of Mykonos in Greece there was a rich young Italian duke who had a car like this, and I always thought if I were rich and successful that's what I would drive. It's a good lesson."

"In what?"

He winked at her. "In disillusionment."

"Are you disillusioned with wealth and success?"

He threw back his head and laughed. "No, just with Italian sports cars, though I've had my eye on a silver Lamborghini one of my customers wants to sell me."

"You're an optimist, then."

"Are you trying to categorize me?"

"I take it you don't like to be labeled."

He grinned at her. "If I said I didn't, then you would just label me one of those people who don't like labels. The trouble with labels is, if they were flattering, I wouldn't mind."

"Oh? What sort of labels are usually pinned on you?"

"According to my parents, obstinate, disrespectful, and impractical. My art teachers labeled me pigheaded, arrogant, but talented, and a customer the other day called me a rude and inconsiderate bastard."

She laughed. "Except for the talented and impractical, which I happen to find endearing qualities, that's not much of a character reference. Tell me, what do your girl friends label you?"

"Brutally honest." He shot a glance at her out of the corner of his dark eyes as he deftly maneuvered the sports car around some traffic. "How would you label yourself?"

"Certainly not honest," she said, thinking of her ruse as a rich heiress.

"That takes a certain amount of honesty to admit. How do other people label you?"

They halted at a signal at the corner of Wilshire and Santa Monica. She looked across the intersection at the fountain that signaled the end of Beverly Hills. For some reason the idea of leaving the Emerald City made her breathe easier. "My sister accuses me of being a dreamy romantic. She's always having to grab hold of my feet and yank me out of the clouds."

"I had a father who tried to do that to me. It's why I left home. You can grow to resent people who are always intent on bursting your bubble."

"I do resent Janet sometimes," she said thoughtfully. "Then again, I can be such a scatterbrain, I don't know what I'd do without her."

"You'd probably do just fine. The bubble bursters of the world don't want to admit it, but the rest of us are able to function perfectly well without them. But I'm curious about your dishonesty. Has this afflicted you long?"

"Don't take that seriously. It was just a joke."

"Was it?"

"You can't be all bad if you're wealthy and successful," she said, trying to change the subject from herself.

"That has nothing to do with my character. It comes from being a brilliant artist."

"I don't suppose anyone has ever called you modest either."

"Never. Show me an artist who is humble, and I'll show you a raving hypocrite. If somebody says to you, 'Your work is wonderful,' and you lower your eyes and say modestly, 'Oh, no, it's terrible,' then they are forced to reassure you all over again. But if you answer, 'Yes, I know it's wonderful,' they can relax. Besides, you've given them a compliment about their own good taste."

"There's a happy medium," she said. "You could simply answer, 'Thank you,' and leave it at that."

"What do you do when someone compliments your poetry?"

"I don't solicit compliments on it. In fact, I hardly ever let anyone see it."

"Why not?"

"I suppose I'm afraid they'll be brutally honest and say they don't like it, or worse, they'll try to be kind and say it's wonderful when they think it's garbage."

He brushed the backs of his fingers fleetingly across her cheek. "You shouldn't let that bother you. I can't tell you the number of people who have looked at my work and called it worse than garbage. If you know inside it's good, that's what matters."

"But it does bother you, doesn't it?" she asked.

The tenderness left his eyes and the fire was back. "Of course it bothers me when people are blind to my work, but if the world is full of ignorant fools, it's not our fault."

Maybe he had the right attitude, she mused. "How long have you been here from Greece?"

"I left Mykonos when I was twenty, fifteen years ago. My mother wasn't pleased, but she's Canadian born and far more understanding about a son who wanted to go his own way. But my father was very old-fashioned. He owned a small tourist hotel and had a place all carved out for me in the business, a little bride for me to marry. All I wanted to do was paint, so I ran off to Paris. It was a very hard time, but I'm glad I did it. Even if I'd failed, it would have been worth it to try."

Raine thought about her poetry, wishing she'd had

the dedication to sacrifice everything for it. "I admire you," she said softly. "I'm afraid if I'd been in your place, I would have buckled under and stayed in Greece."

He gave her a dismissing gesture. "You can say that perhaps because you've never been faced with such a decision."

"How do you know I haven't?"

"Because your own mother even had your poetry published for you. There's nothing wrong with having your family's support."

She leaned back against the plush leather seat and closed her eyes for a moment. "But I think sometimes if you suffer for your art, it means more to you."

"Nonsense. Why do people think all artists should behave like Charlton Heston playing Michelangelo? If an artist has a vision of beauty, it will come out regardless. What he needs most is the time and space to create."

She turned toward him. "And what about artists who don't have the time because they have to make a living?"

"Only one in a thousand artists actually makes a decent living at it," said Ari with a dismissing gesture, "but that doesn't mean you can quit."

"What about you? If you had stayed in Greece and gone into the hotel business, do you think you'd have continued to paint?"

"I thought I had to get away or my father would crush all the creativity in me. But if I'd had to stay for some reason, I think I would have continued somehow. I was burning with the need to be an artist. There were visions of paintings that I had to put down on canvas and that overshadowed everything else. I was ready to starve if I had to."

"You really would have starved to death for your art?"

"To death? No. Of course not. My work is important, but there's no sense in dying for it. Then nobody would ever see it. When times were really bad, I worked in the kitchen of a Greek restaurant on the Rue de Vaugirard where I ate very well. But this talk of starving is making me hungry."

They had driven through Westwood and were now in Santa Monica. "Are you taking me to a picnic at the beach?" she asked playfully.

"To the beach, yes, but not for a picnic." On Ocean Avenue, which ran along the Santa Monica palisade, he turned into a small hotel and gave his car to the attendant.

"There's a restaurant up top," he said, noting her surprised expression. "You didn't really think I'd take you to a hotel this early on in our relationship, did you?"

"I was under the impression we were going to talk about the purchase of a lithograph, not a relationship."

"Let's not put limits on the conversation," he said with a wink as they stepped into an elevator. "It could get interesting."

The restaurant tables were set with blue tablecloths matching the expanse of Pacific Ocean that stretched out below them. As they were shown to their table on the outdoor patio, a woman Raine recognized as a blond television actress began waving frantically to get Ari's attention.

They stopped by her table and she threw her arms dramatically around his neck, kissing him on the cheek. Turning to her friend, she said, "That painting in my bedroom you were admiring the other day. This is the artist!"

Introductions were made and Raine sensed from the way the actress eyed him that it wasn't only his painting that had seen the inside of her bedroom.

Reminding herself that she was there on an assignment from *Buyer Beware,* Raine fought back some highly inappropriate pangs of jealousy. In the back of her head she heard Janet's warning voice. This was one artist who obviously had an infallible artistic sales technique. Double your money, double your fun. It wouldn't surprise her to learn his customer list was ninety-nine percent female.

The waiter adjusted the marine-blue umbrella at their table and took their drink orders. Raine knew she should be looking blasé. If she could afford a ten-thousand-dollar lithograph, these surroundings and beautiful people should be old hat. But it was an effort not to gawk when two heartthrob movie actors drifted by in tennis shorts.

"You'll have to forgive me if I look like Alice in Wonderland," she said with embarrassment. "I'm from Chicago and the sight of movie stars is still something novel."

"I feel the same way. When I was growing up, I used to love American movies, especially the cowboys. Now one of those film cowboys is a customer of mine. I couldn't imagine how my paintings would fit into a ranch, but that's not the way he lived at all. He has a very modern high-tech house—all glass and chrome on top of Bel-Air. It was quite a shock to me."

"Like finding out the truth about Italian sports cars?"

"Not quite that bad," he said with a smile.

She took a deep breath of ocean air and gazed out at the blue expanse of water. "California," she sighed. "This is the way you always picture it to be, with palm trees and movie stars in dark glasses and ocean vistas —and yet when you're here, it's so different."

"But not entirely for you, living in Malibu."

She had almost forgotten that little detail and now wished she'd given a little more thought to her supposed life history. She was no actress, and though she could fool an auto-body repairman, Ari Lekas was another story. He was bound to catch anything amiss. She'd have to be careful.

"I prefer mountains for inspiration," she said dreamily.

"Where do you go?"

"I have a cabin up in . . . Frazier Park." A boyfriend of Janet's had once mentioned having a cabin there.

"Where is that?"

A good question. She had no idea, but evidently he didn't know either. "Out toward San Bernardino," she ventured.

"Why do you prefer mountains?"

"I guess I can relate to pine trees better than palm trees. And standing at the edge of the ocean, you feel awed and insignificant—overwhelmed by the immensity of it."

"And mountains don't overwhelm you?"

"Frazier Park isn't exactly the alps."

"So where would you put my litho, in the mountains or by the sea?"

"In my mother's house at Malibu," she said quickly.

"Then you wouldn't be around much to enjoy it."

"Well, I'd make a special trip in to see it every week," she joked.

"I'd rather you took it with you to the mountains."

"But that would be putting it in a rustic setting, where it wouldn't fit at all."

"Maybe not. What's your cabin like?"

This would be tricky. She'd never been to a cabin anywhere, but she'd seen a few movies. "It's nothing much—just a plain cabin under a lot of pine trees, very isolated from civilization, though I have running water and electricity of course."

"And you go up there all by yourself?"

"Usually."

"Isn't that dangerous?"

"No. I have a shotgun." Now, she really was stretching it. She didn't even know how to squirt a water pistol.

His dark eyebrows rose. "And you don't get lonely?"

She squirmed in her chair. "Well, yes, sometimes, but it's so . . . peaceful." She was thankful the waiter arrived with her spinach quiche. "This is delicious. I just love French food. Did you spend much time in Paris?" She was hoping to get him off the subject of her wilderness cabin.

"I spent four years there. It's a wonderful city. Have you been to Paris?"

"No."

"You must one day. It would inspire your poetry, more than mountains even. Sometimes at dawn I'd stand on the Left Bank across from the Ile St. Louis and just drink it in. Even Marc Chagall said that the light there is like nowhere else on earth. At any time of day, any day of the year, I don't know a more beautiful city. Have you been to Europe?"

Here she was again. It would be unbelievable that a woman of her means had never been to Europe, but she couldn't afford to get tripped up with trying to fake that. Frazier Park was one thing. It was doubtful that many Southern Californians even knew where it was. But if she tried to make up things about Rome or London, he was bound to know she was lying.

"I keep planning trips to Europe, then things come up. I was going last year with my sister, but at the last minute she had to cancel."

"Surely a woman who is not afraid to go to the mountains with no other protection than a shotgun wouldn't mind going to Europe alone?"

"But I don't know the languages, and I'm told it makes officials very nervous if you try to take a shotgun on a transatlantic flight. Tell me, if your lithos are going for ten thousand dollars, how much are your paintings?"

"They start at twenty-five thousand dollars and go up to fifty thousand."

She tried not to look too surprised. "They're so unique, where did you come up with the idea to work in that style?"

He finished the last of his seafood salad and, putting down his fork, said, "When I was a child I was intrigued with prisms and glass objects, the way light breaks into rainbows as it passes through them. The sunlight on Mykonos is very strong, and I would sit outside for hours with colored pencils trying to recreate what I saw. But to tell you now where the paintings come from? I don't know. Where do poems come from? Something will strike me, an emotion, the way the light touches a leaf, and I'll see a painting in my mind. I'll do sketches just to remind myself, but the vision never leaves me until I'm finished."

Raine was only half listening to what he said. She was mesmerized by his hands. There was strength and grace in the long, tapering fingers. "How long does a painting take?"

"How long does a poem take?"

"I've worked on some for years, why?"

"So, you see what a ridiculous question that is. You were going to show me some of your poetry," he reminded her as their plates were cleared.

She suddenly felt self-conscious. "You don't really want to read it, do you?"

"It's not fair that you should see my work and I not be allowed to see yours."

Reluctantly, she reached into her purse and brought out the pamphlet Janet had printed. He opened it immediately and began reading. Watching him, Raine was gripped by such acute embarrassment that she grabbed it away and turned the pages face down. "Why don't you take it with you and read it later at home?"

He gazed at her with understanding and said quietly, "I used to feel that way about my paintings. I hated for anyone to see them and I was terrified of criticism. But you must realize that your work cannot exist only for your own amusement. It's like the old story of the tree falling in the forest. Does it make a sound if nobody is around to hear it?"

"Do you mean to say that it's not poetry if there is nobody around to read it?"

He took her hand, wrapping her fingers around the stem of her wineglass. "Here, you sip some more wine and look out at the ocean while I read. Pretend I'm not here."

Easier said than done. The blue Pacific was a wondrous sight, but she had to steal a glance now and then to see his reactions. There was a fleeting smile, a sparkle in the depths of his black eyes, as he briefly glanced up at her. Was it so bad he thought it was amusing? What was he thinking? She was aching to know. He was almost at the end. She took another sip of wine and focused on the brightly colored sails of a catamaran that was gliding across Santa Monica Bay.

After a small eternity he closed the book, took a deep breath, and faced her. "It's very good, Raine," he said softly. "More than good. It's extraordinary." He took her hand again and laced his long artist's fingers through hers. "The one about the guitarist—how you saw yourself as his guitar, the music and rhythms. How did it go?" He closed his eyes and to her astonishment recited from memory.

> The golden polished wood of my skin
> pressed against your heart
> slender metal strings
> like heartbeats
> wrapped around my waist
> binding me to you . . .

She had read the words to herself a hundred times, but coming from Ari, with the deep, melodious rhythms of his accent, the words took on a new meaning. Her chest felt as though it would break from joy. "You really liked it?" she asked in disbelief.

"Very much. There must have been a guitarist in your life."

She flushed crimson. "This is why I hate to have anyone read it. Right away you took it for granted that it was based on my life."

"Wasn't it?"

Raine looked out at the ocean. "Well, that particular one was. He was a man I . . ."

"A man you loved?" he finished for her.

She nodded.

"What happened?"

"It was unrequited." She tried to sound flippant, but knew she wasn't convincing.

"That other poem about the music that was a seductress," he said quickly.

She smiled sadly. "Oddly, I did some of my best work when I was in the depths of my depression over him. Maybe you do need to suffer to create something beautiful."

"No. You must have only the desire and the inspiration to create something beautiful. May I keep this book?"

"You really want it?"

"I wouldn't ask you for it unless I did." He looked offended that she would dare to question his sincerity. "Will you autograph it for me?"

The thought of inscribing her book of poetry gave her a funny tingle. Instead of an ordinary inscription, she wrote the lines of the poem she'd written about him.

"Nobody has ever written a poem for me before," he said with undisguised delight. "Did you just think it up now?"

"No, it was the night after I saw your work."

"Hah! You see? I was right! My artwork inspired a beautiful poem—there was no suffering at all. Raine." He gazed at her a long moment. "I like your name, like a soft summer rain."

"Why summer?"

"Because in the summer it's very rare and so much more welcome when it does come after a long drought."

He was looking deeply into her eyes. "You must have that litho if it inspires such poetry. I would like to think of you looking at it and putting down more beautiful words."

Raine suddenly fell back to earth with a thud. It certainly was not by chance that he was seductively bringing the subject back around to the purchase. Even Janet, hitting her over the head with a brick, couldn't have made more of a point. The luncheon with the wine included probably put him back fifty dollars, but it was, after all, a tax write-off.

"I would love to see the beach house where it would go," he continued, apparently unaware of her darkening change of mood. "Perhaps I could help you choose a spot for it."

The outrage! She knew there wasn't any honor among thieves, but there should be some among fellow artists. Seducing a customer might be deplorable and underhanded, but using her poetry was downright despicable. Well, he wasn't dealing with a wide-eyed innocent. Two could play at this game. He might not get his sale, but she'd certainly get an article for *Buyer Beware.*

"Perhaps a visit to Malibu could be arranged," she said, slanting a flirtatious gaze up at him. "I'll talk to Mom."

## CHAPTER THREE

Janet put her coffee mug down on her desk and looked up at her sister. "I don't believe what I'm hearing."

Raine's face lit up with a smug smile. "I know you think I'm the most gullible creature on the face of the earth, but I'm not that dumb. Well, maybe a little dumb. For a few minutes there I was really taken in when he started talking about my poetry."

"Now, just because he said he liked your poetry and he was using it as a sales technique doesn't mean your poetry isn't any good," said Janet.

"It just made me so angry that he'd use that—of all things."

"Don't you remember what Mom always used to tell us? 'Pick out something you know the customer loves and give them a compliment on it.' I'll never forget that woman who came in with the most atrocious chartreuse dress on and Mom raved about how beautiful it looked on her."

Raine laughed at the memory. "I asked her how she could tell us not to lie and then lie like crazy about that woman's dress. That's when she sat us both down and gave us that big lecture on all the gray areas between white lies and black lies."

"Oh, yes." Janet leaned back in her chair and closed her eyes. "If somebody asked you how you liked their new dress, you always said you loved it even if you didn't, because they'd already bought it and you'd make them feel terrible if you told the truth. And you were perfectly justified in complimenting customers even if your purpose was to flatter them into a sale because it would make them feel good about themselves. But you could never ever lie about one of the appliances and say that it did things it didn't."

"Don't you sometimes wonder about the kind of lying that we do, though, to get these stories," said Raine.

"Did you feel bad lying to get that job in the nursing home when you found out what they were doing to patients?"

"Not at all."

"Well, there you go. We're sort of like the FBI doing sting operations, and the public is the ultimate benefactor." She gave her sister a quizzical look. "You're not having second thoughts about continuing this story with Ari Lekas, are you?"

Raine sat down at her desk and shuffled through her notes. "In a way, yes, though I don't know why I should."

"What's bothering you?"

"I was just thinking, what if he wasn't really trying to sell me the lithograph?"

"And he mentioned the house as a way to wrangle an invitation from you?" suggested Janet.

"Well, yes," she said uneasily.

"An invitation right into your bedroom just like that actress you told me about. He probably told her his painting would inspire her love scenes."

"I guess you're right."

"You've got to talk to Mrs. Grasset today. I bet she'd loan you her Malibu house for a few hours so you can follow this up."

Raine was sure the publisher of *Buyer Beware* wouldn't want to contribute that much to a story.

"Have McCracken ask Mrs. Grasset for you," Janet persisted.

"No." She threw her notes down on the desk. "I think maybe the best thing is to forget abut the Lekas Gallery. I'll look into some others."

"You're going to do that anyway, but this is such a wonderful angle, you can't let it go. Here's this unscrupulous guy who not only lies about the value of his merchandise, but who literally seduces customers into buying it. You're crazy not to follow through on it. Hey, there's Mrs. Grasset now. Go on over and talk to her."

Raine looked up and saw the woman walk in the door with McCracken.

"It's a perfect time to ask her," whispered Janet. "She even looks like she's in a good mood. Probably had a three-martini lunch."

When Raine hesitated, Janet took her hand and pulled her over to where they were chatting. A tiny, slightly built woman in her fifties, the publisher of *Buyer Beware* was dwarfed by the heavy, balding Bart McCracken. But small as she was, she was known fondly as the Iron Lady, and in the pantheon of consumer dieties, the name Angeline Grasset ranked right up there with Ralph Nader. Her congressional testimonies were legendary for their biting, sarcastic wit. But unlike Ralph Nader, Angeline Grasset had turned consumer crusading into a profitable enterprise with her ever-popular *Buyer Beware,* which could be found at checkout stands of every supermarket.

"Aha!" said McCracken jovially. "There're my two red-haired, blue-blooded star reporters. I was just telling Angie about your Beverly Hills art scam story." Raine was now certain they'd tossed down a few martinis. Bart McCracken wouldn't dare call his boss Angie without a few drinks under his belt.

"I love it," Mrs. Grasset said enthusiastically. "It's fresh, this idea of looking into how the rich get fleeced. In fact, I was just thinking about investing in some art, so it's rather timely."

Raine should have known that Mrs. Grasset, now counting herself among the upper crust, would warm up to this idea of digging into her new stomping ground.

"Raine had lunch with that Beverly Hills artist today," Janet informed them.

"Good," said McCracken. "Did you find out what he was charging for his paintings?"

Why was it that telling them anything made her feel like a traitor? She never felt this way about the autobody shops. "They start at twenty-five thousand dollars."

"Who's this character think he is, Rubens?" McCracken scoffed. "Where does he get off charging those kinds of prices? You gotta find out what he bases that on. It's insane. When are you going to see him again?"

When she didn't answer right away, Janet jumped in. "He wanted to see the house where the lithograph would be hung. We sort of led him to believe that our mother had a beach house in Malibu." Mrs. Grasset raised one penciled eyebrow and Janet continued. "I thought, Mrs. Grasset, that you might be willing to loan Raine your house for a few hours just to help us keep up the front."

"Of course I would! This guy sounds like a real creep with that line about how he's going to double your money. I love to nail phonies like that. Listen, I have a marvelous idea. My husband and I are going up to San Francisco for the weekend. The girl who usually house-sits for us couldn't make it, so we were just going to have a neighbor's kid in to feed the cat. Raine, why don't you come out and house-sit for us? You'd be doing us a favor and you could pretend it was your home and have this artist out. That would erase any doubt he might have that you are who you say you are."

"I wouldn't want to take on the responsibility of looking after your home," she protested.

"You're a lot more responsible than the bratty girl we usually hire. Last time she was there she threw a party. Cleaned up so well we wouldn't have known, but the neighbors told us what went on. You wouldn't throw any parties, would you?"

"Mrs. Grasset, does Raine look like the party-girl type?" McCracken pointed out. He was sobering up quickly if he had already dropped the Angie.

"You don't despise cats, do you?" asked Mrs. Grasset.

"No, I'm crazy about them."

"You may not be after you meet mine," she said under her breath, "but other than that, what do you say to a weekend in Malibu?"

Raine had once been to a staff Christmas party at the Grasset home and she came away with a vivid memory of that fantasy house by the sea. The idea of an entire weekend to herself on the beach was simply too tempting to pass up.

"We have to leave about six Friday night to catch the commuter flight from LAX," she resumed, "so why don't you come by directly after work and we can show you where everything is and introduce you to our charming cat. That'll give you one night to familiarize yourself with the place. Then you can have the artist over Saturday afternoon."

Mrs. Grasset gave her directions, then said, "Too

bad he thinks you're so rich. The best place to pick up information on someone like that is from the inside. I'd love to have you go to work for him, as you did at the nursing home. McCracken, keep it in mind. Maybe one of the other reporters can go down there and apply for a job."

Why she should feel uneasy about continuing the deception, Raine didn't know. It still galled her when she thought of Ari using her poetry as a lure to fish into her bank account.

And yet, what if he had meant what he said?

"Lekas Gallery," he said when he answered the phone.

"Hi, it's Raine."

"Summer rain," he said intimately. "What are you doing?"

"Isn't the question, how are you?"

"The answer to that is always fine. I'd rather know what you're up to."

"You probably wouldn't."

"Try me."

"I was just wondering if you'd like to come by the Malibu house Saturday afternoon."

"I would very much, but Saturday is impossible. It's a busy day in Beverly Hills. The gallery is usually packed and I have to attend a dinner party that night at the home of a customer. How about Sunday afternoon?"

The Grassets were coming back Sunday afternoon so that was out of the question. "No, I'm busy Sunday. Well, maybe some other time." She actually felt a great relief at being able to tell McCracken her meeting with Ari couldn't be arranged after all.

"We're both creative," he said, "let's think creatively. What about Friday night?"

"But it would be dark, and you couldn't see how the natural light would affect the lithograph," she said quickly.

"I have a good imagination."

"I bet you do."

He laughed. "And if I get there before sunset, I'll still be able to tell. Malibu faces west, so there will still be sunlight until at least seven. Why don't I come by around six?"

And run smack into the Grassets just as they were leaving? "Make it six thirty," she suggested.

"Fine, and I'll take you to dinner."

"Oh, that's not necessary."

"It is. Unless you are still romanticizing about starving for your poetry. Now, tell me how I get there."

Fortunately, Raine had just taken the directions down and repeated verbatim what Mrs. Grasset had told her.

As she told her sister later, "Dinner wasn't something I had counted on."

"It's great—that much more opportunity to pump him for information about the gallery," said Janet.

"But a little candlelight with Ari Lekas in Malibu could be a highly combustible combination."

"We'll see if we can't find you a designer dress of sequined asbestos for the occasion."

Since it was only Tuesday, she had some time to do more research on the story. The first line of attack was to investigate other art galleries to see if their prices were significantly different from his. If Janet and McCracken were correct, art prices should get lower the farther away one moved from the Emerald City. Checking geographically, she decided to begin her search on the periphery of Beverly Hills, then move out.

Her first gallery was near the design center on Melrose Avenue and specialized in the French painter Cordouan. A toupeed aging man whose facelift was so tight his expression seemed cast in cement confided, "Cordouan's work is a steal right now."

"At thirty thousand dollars a painting?" asked Raine.

"My dear, the man is in his eighties. How much longer can he go on producing? If you bought a painting at thirty thousand and he died tomorrow, it would double in value overnight. Look what happened when Picasso died."

Here was yet another double-your-money offer. If the art market was really that hot, why would people waste their time with stocks and bonds and real estate?

"Have you ever heard of a painter named Ari Lekas?" asked Raine.

"Aristotle Lekas? Very big in New York. Quite the rage, in fact, though that doesn't mean much. New Yorkers will jump on anything they're told is innovative. I once attended an opening in Soho of an ex-mechanic who had gotten drunk and disassembled an old Harley-Davidson motorcycle and welded the parts together. They were selling the pieces for ten thousand dollars each." He shook his head and sighed. "And people were buying."

"I notice you don't handle any of Lekas's work."

"Nobody does in L.A. Lekas keeps everything to himself in his gallery on Rodeo Drive." The man made Ari sound downright miserly about it. "Oh, wait a minute. I did hear a rumor the other day about a gallery that just opened on the Wilshire Miracle Mile that had a few of his pieces."

"Do you recall the name?"

"French name." He thought a minute. "Yes, Prasteau."

"What do you think of his work?" she pressed.

The man shrugged. "It's very good if you like contemporary art, though I think if you're looking for a solid investment, you're better off with Cordouan. Lekas is still young and he's bound to be producing for a good many more years."

"What about his lithographs? He only does editions of six. I'd think if you got one of the last available, you'd also double back your investment."

The man's face, pulled as taut as it was, showed no expression, but one eyelid drooped disdainfully. "Yes, perhaps, if he's hot enough, but there is rarely such a thing as being the last available. After all, they're still selling Rembrandts. And unless Lekas dies tomorrow in a car accident, his works will be sold and resold on the open market for quite some time. Believe me, you're always better off financially with an artist who is dead or nearly dead."

"Do you think a Lekas painting is worth twenty-five thousand dollars?"

The man shrugged again. "If that's what he's getting these days. Look at the motorcycle sculptor, and he probably couldn't even draw a straight line with a monkey wrench. You charge whatever the market will bear. If people are willing to pay it, of course it's worth it. But artists run in fads. Next year Lekas may go the way of Nehru jackets. Cordouan, at least, is well established, the last of the greats of this century along with Picasso. You can't go wrong, and I have it from an impeccable source his eyesight is failing. Even if he lives another ten years, which I assure you is unlikely, he won't be producing much longer."

What a ghoul! The man actually seemed to relish lurking around like a vulture waiting for artists to crumble and die. What was he running, an art gallery or a funeral parlor?

Raine was glad to get back out into the fresh air of the street. But after several other gallery visits, she began to realize that the mortician's view of art was not unusual. Most gallery owners seemed more interested in handling someone who had departed this life than an artist just making a mark on it. Though a few brave souls specialized in new talent, they couldn't demand the same prices. So where did Ari Lekas fit in?

He was obviously in vogue, charging and getting prices equal to well-established artists like Cordouan. Then again, the motorcycle welder hadn't done too shabbily either. This was not an easy market to pin down. Her gut feeling was that Ari Lekas would never go out of style, and since he was in some highly respectable permanent collections, she wasn't the only one with that opinion.

Ari's work had an emotional impact, an exciting, fanciful flair that was at once original and dynamic, whereas Cordouan's pretty, sentimental paintings were only echoes of the last lyric strains of French Impressionism.

Since the man had mentioned that the Prasteau Gallery carried some Lekas work, Raine decided to pay a visit. It was located off the lobby of a new high-rise office building. The gallery's bold abstract paintings and modernistic sculptures fit in well with the steel and glass structure.

At first Raine was stunned by the beauty of the woman who greeted her and introduced herself as Nicole Prasteau. It was hard to pinpoint her age. It could have been anywhere from early thirties to mid-forties. Her ash-blond hair was pulled tightly away from a smooth patrician face and knotted into an elegant chignon at the nape of her neck. In her tailored beige suit with padded shoulders and white silk blouse, she had the perfect appearance to inspire a jittery first-time art investor with confidence. That confidence would be crucial. This was not a woman content to deal with the dead or nearly dead. More than one of the works on display in her gallery could have been created by the mad motorcycle mechanic. Even a seasoned art critic would be hard put to say if the paintings and sculptures were works of junk or genius, but they were unquestionably unusual.

Perhaps she was prejudiced, but Raine thought the Lekas paintings were by far the best work in the gallery, and she found herself drawn to them as irresistibly as before.

"The one you are looking at is by Aristotle Lekas," said Nicole with a French accent as she walked toward Raine. She rattled off his credentials, naming the permanent collections he was in and a few of his better-known patrons. Raine was amused to hear the name of the actress she had met included. "I have the only gallery outside his own in Los Angeles that carries his work," she said with pride.

"How is that?"

"I deal only in the best," she answered simply.

Raine walked around the room and eventually came back to the Lekas painting. "I was in his gallery not long ago and was very impressed, but his prices seemed a bit steep."

Nicole's glossed lips tilted upward. "You are very wise to shop around before buying. My prices are quite a bit lower than his. Of course I don't have all the overhead of a Rodeo Drive gallery."

Not knowing exactly how paintings were priced, she decided to ask about the lithograph. Since they were all the same, it would be easier to make a price comparison. "There was a particular lithograph I saw in

Beverly Hills. It was sort of like this painting, but if you stood toward the side, you could see a woman's face in it." She drew it in the air.

"I know exactly which one you describe. Gorgeous, isn't it?"

"Breathtaking."

"One of my customers has the third edition in her private collection. How much is Ari asking now?"

"Ten thousand dollars."

Nicole raised her eyebrows in such a way that Raine was prompted to ask if she thought it was overpriced.

"I hate to speak disparagingly about another gallery, but I must be honest with you. I hate to see anyone get taken. Ten thousand is terribly inflated."

"If you don't mind my asking, how much did your customer pay?"

"I sold it to her for forty-five hundred two years ago, and I think she would let it go for five thousand."

Raine's mouth dropped open. "You mean in two years it only increased five hundred dollars in value?"

"I suppose Mr. Lekas told you it would double as soon as you bought it."

"Why yes, he did."

"He is living a fantasy. Ten thousand is out of line, but twenty thousand for that litho is preposterous. However, you must realize that if you were to buy hers for five thousand, you could easily turn around and make three thousand dollars very fast."

"You're going a little fast for me. How do you figure?"

"If you wanted to give it back to me to sell on consignment, I could sell it for eight thousand, that's two thousand cheaper than the one in the Lekas gallery, and you'd make a three-thousand-dollar profit. Not quite double your money, but close."

"What about your commissions?"

"The standard ten percent."

Raine did some quick mental calculations. "That comes to eight hundred, dropping my profit down to twenty-two hundred, not three thousand."

"It's still not a bad rate of return. You'd never see it at a bank."

"But why would your customer sell it for such a low profit when she, too, could get eight thousand?"

"It may take a while to sell, and she's getting a divorce and would like to get cash for as many things as she can very quickly. But this painting I have here. He has one quite similar and I'm sure he's asking at least thirty thousand for it. My price is sixteen thousand, almost half."

Raine's head was spinning with calculations. She wished Janet were here. She was always much better at unraveling financial things. But one thing was certain. Even car bumpers didn't fluctuate by this much. She was onto a good consumer story.

"Why do you suppose Lekas is charging so much?"

"As I say, I hate to speak disparagingly about another gallery, but his prices are just the sort of thing that gives reputable galleries a bad name. Of course he is selling his own work, and with his ego he would have an inflated idea of its worth. Heaven only knows how he gets those prices, but he is very good-looking, with all that Mediterranean charm, and he knows just how to use those dark eyes to devastating effect. Most of his patrons are women and they fall all over him, though I understand he entertains them lavishly to make a sale."

The look in Nicole's eyes left no doubt about how he entertained them. Here was the confirmation of everything she suspected. The thought of him tossing her poems in the trash, laughing about his latest conquest and sale, made her burn with anger.

"You've been kind enough to be honest with me," said Raine. "So I'll be honest with you, Ms. Prasteau. I'm not really in the market for artwork. I'm writing an article for the consumer magazine *Buyer Beware*. We're doing a whole series on how rich people can get ripped off, and I've been investigating art galleries in particular. Mr. Lekas's prices did seem rather inflated, so I've been checking around."

Nicole's smile widened, but her gray eyes remained cool. "Well, I'm happy to help in any way I can. Please don't quote me, but I hate to see somebody as unscrupulous as Ari Lekas in business. People like that think that just because you're shopping in Beverly Hills you can afford the moon. Maybe you can, but there are important principles at stake."

Since Nicole had been so helpful, Raine approached several other galleries with the straight story of who she was and what she was doing, but outspoken art dealers like Nicole Prasteau, ready to discredit a colleague, were almost nonexistent.

"It's like trying to find a doctor to testify against another doctor in a malpractice suit," McCracken told her Friday as he looked over her notes. "They're all very careful to protect each other. That's why you can always get more information out of people if you tell them you're anything but a reporter. They'll tell their plumbers anything, but the minute you say you're a reporter, they think they're going to be raked over the coals on *60 Minutes*." He tapped his pencil on her notebook. "Some damn good stuff here, Walken. I had no idea this business was so shifty and complex."

"Neither did I. I thought you went into a gallery and bought a painting just as you went into a supermarket and bought a loaf of bread. But with all these buy-back options and complex financing schemes, it's no wonder people stick to something simple like the stock market."

"Yeah, art dealing makes playing the horses look like a sure thing. You gonna see that painter tonight at the Grassets'?"

She glanced at her watch. "Yes, and I'd better run or I'm going to be late."

Her sister was coming in just as she was flying out the door. "Got your asbestos dress all pressed?"

"Heavens no. The wrinkled look is in."

Later that night, Raine was to wonder if an asbestos dress might have been a good idea after all. Then again, even a coat of armor was no protection if your adversary knew exactly where you were vulnerable.

# CHAPTER FOUR

Raine figured that with rush-hour traffic it would take at least an hour to get to Malibu, but there was unusually heavy traffic on the Santa Monica Freeway, and the Pacific Coast Highway was bumper to bumper with people going away for the weekend. It was almost six thirty by the time she arrived at the Grassets' house. Raine prayed that Ari wouldn't also be waiting on the doorstep.

As the Grassets were already late for their commuter fight to San Francisco, there was barely time to show her how to double lock the doors. Just as she sat down at the kitchen table to catch her breath, the doorbell rang. Smoothing a hand over her frazzled hair, she flew to the door and fumbled with the complicated locks.

"Hi there," she said, out of breath. Having just come from the *Buyer Beware* office, she was still in slacks and a T-shirt. Ari was in a dark suit and tie. "I'm not quite ready," she apologized. "Just got here myself a few minutes ago."

"Relax, I'm in no hurry and you look wonderful."

The way his dark-eyed gaze swept over her would have made her melt under any other circumstances, but knowing how bedraggled she looked, it was obvious he was already geared to his sales pitch.

As they walked into the living room, she saw the

same appreciative gaze wander over the plush decor and sweeping vista of a spectacular Pacific Ocean sunset. He really thinks he's hooked a live one, Raine mused.

"It's a beautiful home," he said. "Where's your mother?"

"San Francisco for the weekend." She regretted saying that as soon as it was out of her mouth. It would have been wiser to say she'd be back later so he wouldn't get the idea he might be welcome to spend the night. "Do you see a place for your lithograph?"

He walked toward the window. "Somewhere along this wall, perhaps, but I must study the house. It doesn't necessarily have to be in a living room."

She was sure the actress could attest to that. "But I know my mother. She would want to display such beautiful work where everyone could see it. Well, you go ahead and look around while I go upstairs and get dressed."

"Take your time. I'm enjoying the view."

She started to leave, then realized how rude it was not to offer him a drink. "Would you care for something to drink while you wait?"

"That would be very kind. A Scotch on the rocks if you have it."

Raine glanced around furtively. Where would the Grassets keep their liquor? She tried to think back to the party. Though she seemed to recall a professional bartender in the corner of the living room serving drinks, it must have been a portable bar because that space was now occupied by a glass étagère. The Grassets had to have a liquor cabinet in the kitchen. She only hoped they didn't keep it locked so a cleaning lady or house-sitter wouldn't slip in and take a nip.

"I'll go fix it and bring it out to you," she said.

"I'll help you," he offered, following ner into the kitchen.

He had picked a fine time to be helpful. She had never seen so many cabinets in her life, and none of them seemed to contain liquor. "Forgive me, I can't remember where my mother keeps the liquor. It used to be here," she mumbled, flinging open a cabinet door that was filled with canned goods. "But then she had a big housecleaning last month and rearranged everything. She does that all the time, kind of an organizational fanatic. Does the same things with her closets. It drives me and Janet crazy."

She finally found the liquor and was gratified to spy a bottle of excellent twelve-year-old Scotch. Not bad for a cost-conscious consumer activist, Raine mused. Ari even complimented her mother's good taste.

She fumbled only slightly with the ice cube tray and managed, hands shaking, to present him with his drink. Just then she heard a scratching at the back door. The cat. She was supposed to feed the cat before she left. Opening the door, Raine let in a huge brindle-striped cat that gave her a skeptical look. "Come here, kitty kitty," she said sweetly.

The cat hissed at her and walked over to Ari. "What's your name, pretty cat?" He drew out the syllables in what sounded like a purr and the cat responded by rubbing against his legs. He picked it up, cradling it against his chest. The cat purred so loudly she could hear it across the room.

Definitely a female cat, Raine surmised. "Her name is Eloise," she said, thinking it was as good a name as any. "Eloise, do you want your dinner?"

The word dinner seemed to spark an interest and Eloise, digging her claws into her new friend, leaped back onto the floor and began yowling loudly, rubbing back and forth against the refrigerator. Luckily Raine had run across the cat food while searching for the Scotch.

"Eloise is a strange name for a male cat," Ari commented as Raine hunted for a garbage can in which to toss the empty can.

"Mom has a strange sense of humor," she said nervously, wondering how she could have missed that important detail. Now was the time to stage an escape. "Uh, why don't you go ahead and scan the living room for a suitable place for your litho while I take a shower and change."

Grabbing her suitcase in the hall, she ran upstairs and after opening only two doors, one of which was the linen closet, she found the guest bedroom and adjacent bathroom.

As she stripped off her clothes, she wondered how much longer she'd be able to pull off this charade before he began to suspect there was something fishy. And was it worth it? Maybe the wisest thing would be to march downstairs right now and confess. Well, maybe not exactly this very minute, she thought as she caught a glimpse of herself stark naked on her way into the bathroom and the shower.

Last month while they were down at the clothing mart, Janet had talked her into buying a white gauze dress sample from a famous Moroccan designer. It had a fringed low-cut neckline and billowy sleeves. Since she generally went in for a more tailored look, she wondered at the time when she'd ever wear something like it, but a dinner date with a Greek god seemed a fitting occasion for a Mediterranean dress.

Letting her auburn hair hang in soft waves around her shoulders, she took a thin piece of the same gauze material and, imitating a fashion model she'd seen wearing a similar dress in Vogue, wrapped it around her head several times and let the rest of the material hang down like a ribbon. To finish the effect she applied teal eyeliner and smoothed the same shade of eyeshadow all the way up to her eyebrows. No, too dramatic, she decided, and toned down the shadow by a third.

Twirling around in front of the mirror, she smiled at herself. Not in the least asbestos. This was a look that would attract flames, not repel them. Raine felt like a naughty little girl dressed up in a devil costume for a Sunday school play.

Well, this was sort of like a play. She had fabricated a ruse, a setting, and a persona, and suddenly, instead of feeling uncomfortable with it, she was bubbling with excitement. Did an actress feel this way just before going on stage?

Ari was standing out on the balcony when she came downstairs. As he turned, he saw the red-gold light of the sunset catch her hair and paint the white dress golden. She might as well have risen up out of the sea foam, he thought. All the fiery beauty he had suspected was illuminated with dazzling intensity by the setting sun.

Leaning up against the railing, he took another sip of Scotch and tried to steady his heartbeat as she came toward him. This house, the dress, her hair . . . never in his life had such a magnificently planned lie been fabricated to seduce him. Not even Nicole Prasteau had been this good.

And he had learned his lesson well from Nicole. No woman went to this much trouble without some ulterior motive. Sex was not the payoff in this case, it was only a means to an end.

What was Raine really after? God help me, he thought as he smiled bitterly, whatever she wants, I'm just liable to give it to her.

A breeze off the ocean was blowing his golden hair

onto his forehead. His sculpted features stood out in stark relief against the backdrop of the vermilion-streaked sky as his dark gaze swept over her. For a moment she thought he looked angry as he took a sip of Scotch, then vastly amused. Once again, Raine felt like the naughty little girl in the devil suit, but one who had just tripped over her tail at a crucial moment, and though the audience was too polite to laugh out loud, it was nonetheless getting a good, stifled chuckle from the pratfall.

"It should go here," he said, coming inside and indicating the wall over the couch. "But your mother will have to move this other painting."

"I'm sure she won't mind. You know how she loves to rearrange things." If he only knew. Her mother hadn't so much as moved an ashtray, except to dust, in over twenty-five years.

"How beautiful you look in white," he said softly. "And I like your hair down on your shoulders." He picked up a curl and twisted it around his long fingers. "Such an unusual dark color of red."

Raine trembled and moved away from him. "It was bright red when I was a child, but as I got older it darkened. The kids in my kindergarten class used to make fun of me and call me 'carrot top' until my sister Janet trounced them. She was in the fourth grade and a seasoned pro at dealing with that kind of ridicule. She told me that redheads have a reputation for terrible tempers and advised me that if I wanted to get through grammar school in one piece, I'd better cultivate the myth."

"Did you?"

"I tried biting a few kids when I was angry, but never really got the hang of intimidation. I think it's something you're born with."

"And there really isn't any need to stand up for

yourself when you've got a tough older sister who will fight your battles for you," he remarked.

"I'd never really thought of it before, but I guess you're right. Janet was always coming to my rescue, and still is. We were regular little tomboys. Our mother would send us off to school in crisp ironed dresses and we'd come home with our hems hanging, our knees skinned, and covered with dirt. Mom once took some before-and-after school pictures that are a riot."

"It's hard to imagine you as a tomboy. Especially looking at you tonight. I'd love to see those pictures."

"Oh, I don't have any with me."

"Your mother has no pictures of you as a little girl?"

"Uh, no. She doesn't believe in family photographs around. Another one of her quirks."

"But what about those photos in the den?"

Raine bit her lower lip nervously. She didn't even know there was a den. "Oh, I forgot about those. She just had some framed up last month. I guess as she gets older, she gets more sentimental."

"Let's go see, you must be in one of those pictures."

"How about if we take a look when we get back from dinner," she said, hoping he would have forgotten by then. "I'm absolutely famished."

He glanced at his watch. "We should go. I made reservations for eight, and by the time we drive up the canyon it will almost be that time. When we come back, you can show me the pictures."

"Where are we going?" She once again fumbled with the double locks and searched for the switch for the outdoor lights.

"There's a beautiful little restaurant hidden up in Malibu Canyon," he said as he located the switch for her. "I think the poet in you will like it."

63

He left the top of his sports car down so that they could enjoy the warm night, the tangy fragrance of the ocean mingling with that wild, pungent chaparral of the canyon. She took a deep breath and leaned back to see the sky. There were few lights on the winding road, and this far out of Los Angeles the sky was velvety black, sparkling with stars.

"I love the names of the Los Angeles canyons," she said dreamily and recited them, "Malibu Canyon, Laurel Canyon, Topanga Canyon, Coldwater Canyon. Then there are the passes, Sepulveda Pass, Cahuenga Pass. It makes you think that not really so long ago, the only inhabitants were the Indians and the coyotes. Did you know that the main god of the Southern California Indians was the Great Coyote?"

"The coyotes still own the hills," said Ari. "I live in Laurel Canyon and hear them yipping and howling at night. It's what I like about Los Angeles. You are in civilization, but not too far away is the sea and these wonderful, wild mountains."

Just before reaching the ridge, they turned into a driveway. Nestled amid sycamore and oak trees was an old Victorian restaurant with a gingerbread facade. A sign in front of the building proclaimed the name of the restaurant to be Moonbeams.

"This used to be a stagecoach stop," said Ari. "The owners are friends of mine. They found the building abandoned and ready to be torn down and decided to renovate it into a restaurant." In keeping with the turn-of-the-century theme were red-flocked wallpaper and ornate chandeliers. Each of the rooms had only a few tables. They were shown to a secluded booth paneled in dark oak.

As she had suspected, soft candlelight and Ari Lekas were a heady combination. Watching the golden light flicker across his chiseled features, reflected in his midnight eyes, listening to the deep, melodic tones of his voice, she felt herself lulled into a magical trance.

When he spoke to her, his attention was riveted on her eyes as though nothing else in the world mattered, and he punctuated what he said by touching her arm or cheek lightly. Suddenly aware that his hard thigh was pressed against hers, she knew she should pull away, but several glasses of Châteauneuf du Pape had worn down her resistance.

It was all she could do to remind herself that if he hadn't been convinced she had an extra ten thousand dollars, she wouldn't be there with him at all.

After a sinfully delicious meal of roast duck in raspberry sauce and an utterly voluptuous slice of chocolate mousse pie, she was sipping an after-dinner drink of Rémy Martin cognac when he took her hand. "I've read your poetry over and over again, Raine. It's even more beautiful and more profound than I originally thought. So many images are overlaid one on the other. Have you thought of publishing more?"

She was entranced by the way her slender hand fit into his large tanned one, the way he was tracing the outline of her fingers. "That wasn't really published. Janet just took some of my poems and had them typeset. There were only about fifty copies made."

"I thought your mother had the poems published for you."

Damn the Châteauneuf, or was it the Rémy? "My mother and Janet did it together."

"And your father? You never speak about him."

"He passed away a few years ago."

"What did he think of your poetry?"

"I never showed it to him."

"Why not?"

"There were things in there . . . well, a father just wouldn't understand."

"What kind of work did your father do?"

"Oh, investments and things. It was mostly a matter of managing what had been left to him." It wasn't entirely a lie. Gunnar Walken had inherited a fierce wealth of pride from his Indiana farming parents and had carved out a comfortable, though far from lavish, living for his family with his appliance store in Chicago.

Ari leaned back against the booth and closed his eyes for a moment. "I used to wish my father could understand what I was trying to do. None of my family does, really. The one I'm closest to, my younger sister, came to visit me in Los Angeles a few months ago. She understood Rodeo Drive and Beverly Hills and how that stood for success, but the work itself meant nothing."

"You're doing so well. Somebody must be understanding."

He smiled sadly and kissed the tips of her fingers. "Unfortunately, few people buy art because they love or understand it. One of my customers told me she owns an original painting by the Renaissance artist Sebastian del Piombo, a protégé of Michelangelo. It's an exquisite painting and she keeps it in a vault in Paris, waiting for it to appreciate in value. Like a stock certificate."

"People like that should be locked up in vaults instead of their paintings," Raine said indignantly. "It should be against the law to hide masterpieces from the public. I'm curious, though. How exactly do you set a value on your own work?" She hoped he'd had enough wine himself to loosen up and to give her some information for her article.

"Ah, that is not a simple question. Everything comes into account. You consider how long it took you to paint it, what your feelings were about it, how large it is, but in the end, you must stand back and look at the painting itself and judge it against everything else you've done."

He wasn't being very explicit and that still didn't explain how he could come up with those exorbitant prices. "Please don't be offended, but why twenty-five thousand dollars instead of twenty-five hundred?"

"It's very simple," he said with a shrug. "You charge what people are willing to pay."

"Aren't you afraid somebody will undercut you?"

"Only two other galleries carry my work; both are in New York and we agree on prices. As soon as I sell one of my lithos, for example, I call them and they double the prices on theirs."

It seemed impossible he wouldn't know about Nicole Prasteau's gallery even though it was relatively new in town. Nicole certainly gave the impression she knew him well, perhaps intimately. It had to be that he simply didn't want anyone to know there was another gallery in town where his work was for sale at a lower price than he was charging.

"But doesn't some of your work eventually turn up again on the open market?"

"Not much. When I or my dealers sell a work to a customer, we usually maintain a limited option to resell the work on consignment."

"I don't think I understand."

"Well, if you were to buy the litho, and let's say within the year you wanted to resell it, you'd bring it back to me and I'd sell it for you."

"And take a commission."

"Any gallery would, but you'd be most likely to get the best price from me because I have a vested interest in maintaining the value."

"And what if you decided not to sell it?"

"That's why we'd have a limited option agreement.

I'd have only so many months to make the sale, then you'd be free to take it wherever you pleased."

"If I owned that lithograph, I would never sell it," she said honestly.

He gazed at her for a long moment. "I still can't believe it. How is it that you walk into my gallery one day out of nowhere and immediately understand my work, almost better than I do? Raine, you are a woman of unusual insights. You must publish more than fifty copies of your poems."

"It's not that easy," she said with a sigh. "The going rate for poems these days is zero. There's not much of a market for them."

"You can't let it discourage you. I was told the same thing about paintings. My professors in Paris advised me to work smaller because small paintings were easier to display, store, and ship. What reasons to dedicate your life to something! You must do what you have to do whether it's commercial or not."

She thought of her long hours at *Buyer Beware*. "Not if you have to keep a roof over your head."

He raised a dark eyebrow. "I thought you didn't work."

"Oh, I don't," she said nervously. "But it's a constant battle with my mother, who thinks I should be out earning my own way. She's convinced that working builds character and all that."

"Will you let me read your other poems?"

"You really want to see them?"

"Very much."

He looked so sincere she could almost believe him. He took her chin in his hand, rubbing his thumb lightly across her lips. "You think I'm simply flattering you because I want to make love to you?"

"No," she said with a smile, the cognac making her

bold. "I think you're flattering me to sell me your litho."

A muscle in his jaw tightened, and his dark eyes narrowed as he dropped his hand. "I'll get the check and we'll go." Did she take him for a blithering idiot? He knew she wasn't in the market for that litho. But what was she in the market for? That was what worried him.

They drove back down the canyon in an uneasy silence. He hadn't denied her accusation. Was that the same as admitting she had been right?

She didn't know what difference it made if he really liked her poetry or not. Her job was to get information for her article, and in that regard she hadn't done much more than to establish that he didn't let potential customers know there was a competitive gallery operating.

In the delightful haze of wine, candlelight, and Ari, she hadn't gleaned anything significant. When they pulled up in front of the Malibu house, she quickly opened her car door, thinking he would be anxious to be rid of her now that she knew what he was about. "No need to get out," she told him. "I'll be all right."

"If you can figure out how to work those double locks," he muttered.

He was right. She couldn't have managed the locks without him. As soon as the door was open, she said, "Thanks for a nice dinner. I'll . . . uhm . . . call you if I'm interested in the litho."

He walked past her into the house. "It's not that late. I thought we might take a walk down the beach."

"I'm very tired."

"We have some things to say to each other."

"The only thing we have to say to each other is good night."

"Take off your shoes," he said.

"Why?"

"Because you don't want to ruin them in the sand."

"Ari, I'm not going for a walk on the beach with you."

He opened the door to the terrace and a breeze of warm ocean air swept into the house. Ari and the entire Pacific Ocean seemed to be in a conspiracy to make her walk on the beach. "Oh, all right."

They both kicked off their shoes, and Ari left his jacket draped over the couch. They took the narrow wooden stairs that wound down through the boulders to the beach.

Moonlight painted her dress a pale blue, matching the lacy caps of the waves as they broke and swept up over the cool, damp sand, caressing their bare ankles.

"You look beautiful in the moonlight, Raine," he said softly. Wrapping his strong arms around her waist, he pulled her close. Alarms were clanging inside her like smoke detectors, but it was too much to ask fire resistance of a simple poet, she thought wildly, as she lifted her face to his.

His lips were softer than she imagined, and his kiss was as gentle as a moonbeam. She ran her fingers through his thick blond hair while his large hands moved over her rib cage and his thumbs rubbed lightly at the sides of her breasts. Trembling, she became pliant in his arms, as he moved his lips across her cheek and down her neck. Then, taking her shoulders in his strong hands, he looked down steadily into her eyes. "Now, Raine, the truth about yourself."

"I'm a poet," she said dreamily, and lifted her lips to his again.

"That's the only true thing you've ever told me about yourself." He took a step back from her, gripping her shoulders. "Everything else is a lie."

## CHAPTER FIVE

She broke away from him and walked quickly down the beach. He followed and with a few long strides was beside her. Impatient now to get to the bottom of the deception, he grabbed her wrist and swung her around. "That isn't your mother's house any more than it is mine. I'd venture to say you hadn't even been in that house before today."

"Not true," she said defiantly, and twisting out of his grip, she kicked a plume of water out to sea. "I was there once for a Christmas party."

"What's the rest of the story, Raine, or is that not even your real name?" Gone was the tenderness of the kiss. There was a hard edge to him now that frightened her.

"Of course it's my name. Why would I make up a name like that?"

"With some of the lies that have come from your lips I wouldn't put anything past you."

"You've checked everything I've said for accuracy?" she asked sarcastically.

"Frazier Park isn't anywhere near San Bernardino, for one thing."

"Oh, where is it?"

"Up toward Bakersfield off Interstate Five."

"So I was off by a few hundred miles."

"Do you not even have a cabin?"

"I've never been in a cabin and I don't own a shotgun either." She looked up at him coolly. "And if you're expecting any more information from me, you're out of luck."

"I've had it with your lies. Before tonight is over I want to know everything about you." The woman was exasperating. Civility was quickly turning into anger.

"Isn't this moral indignation a little misplaced? I'm the one who should be mad at you for using my poetry to seduce me into buying your lithograph."

His dark eyes flashed dangerously and suddenly she was down on the sand, her arms pinned over her head and his face was very close. "Damn it, Raine, everything I said about your poetry was true."

"About as true as my cabin in Frazier Park."

"Raine . . ." Seeing her beneath him so vulnerable and beautiful made him forget his rage. How could he stay angry with this woman who was so enticing, so appealing? He looked into her eyes for a moment, eyes that glared up at him with an almost childlike defiance, and then Ari smiled. He wanted her despite her lies. His lips came down on hers, harshly at first. He felt her tense, trying not to respond, but finally she gave in. He let go of her wrists. His large hands stroked downward over her breasts and belly. A shock wave pulsed through her, and despite her efforts to remain immobile, Raine found herself breathlessly arching to him.

He lifted his head and looked down at her. "We could have so much," he said softly. "Why do you hold back from me?"

"What difference does it make?" she answered, struggling in a halfhearted way. "If I buy your litho, you don't need to know anything about me except that my check is good."

He couldn't resist giving her a gentle nip. "And I

suspect that check would be bouncing from here to Frazier Park."

"Try Mozambique," she said a little petulantly.

He entwined his long fingers in her red hair and kissed the sides of her mouth lightly. "Let's start slowly. Whose house is that?"

Raine hesitated a few seconds. She briefly contemplated trying to fabricate another lie but decided that was useless at this point. "A publisher's," she finally admitted.

He looked at her suspiciously. "You're involved with this publisher?"

"In a manner of speaking. That's how I make my living," she answered, deliberately trying to make him misunderstand.

Pulling the already low-cut neckline even lower, he exposed a breast, and encircling it with his large hand, he kissed the tip, drawing it hard with his mouth. She moaned and entwined her fingers in his thick hair. He suddenly stopped and looked up at her. "So this publisher keeps you, is that it?"

"No!" She squirmed out from under him and, sitting up, covered her breast. This was going too far, too fast. What did Ari want? Was he angry at her or was this some kind of game? She couldn't tell. His mood seemed too changeable. "The publisher is a she and nobody keeps me but myself."

Grinning, he pulled her back down beside him. "So what are you doing in this house?"

"I wish I had some really good, gritty story to feed your already-overworked imagination, but the truth is I'm just house- and cat-sitting for the weekend."

Watching her eyes, he pulled the dress down again, this time over both breasts. Wetting the tip of his finger with his tongue, he drew tiny circles around the dark nipples. Raine's lips parted and her breathing grew ragged. She knew she should resist him, but couldn't bring herself to do it.

"Where do you live?" he asked.

"Burbank," she moaned.

"And what do you do for a living?"

"Where did you learn your interrogation techniques?"

He smiled. "Answer my question."

His caresses were making her helpless. All the fight had drained out of her. As he slipped his hand up under her dress, she gasped and whispered, "How can I answer any question when you're . . ."

"What do you do for a living, Raine?"

She made a feeble attempt to move his hand, but it wouldn't budge, and she wasn't sure she really wanted it to. "You don't give up, do you?"

"Not when I want something badly enough."

"All right, I'll tell you, if you promise to stop this."

His hand was quiet as he waited.

"I'm a writer."

His large hand moved around her hips and stroked the backs of her thighs. All her nerve endings were crying out to her. "What kind of things do you write?"

"I don't think you want to know," she managed to say, though her mouth was so dry she could barely speak. "And I thought you were going to stop."

"Not yet." Cupping her buttocks, he pulled her against him, and feeling how aroused he was, she reasoned her best defense against his questions was to get his mouth busy with something more pleasurable. At least she told herself that was why she pressed her lips against his. Resolute, he wouldn't open his mouth to hers, and his deliberate caresses continued, sweeping roughly and intimately over her whole body.

"What do you write?" he pressed her.

"Hard-core pornography."

He paused for a moment, and drawing back, he looked at her, his dark eyes very wide. Then he burst into a deep, bellowing laugh and rolled onto his back. "You do come up with some amazing stories."

"You like that one?"

"Immensely."

"You don't think I'm capable of it?"

His hand wandered insistently over the curve of her breasts. "Some of your poetic metaphors are very erotic, but pornography doesn't leave as much as you do to the imagination."

"Would you believe that I write maintenance manuals for Boeing Seven-forty-sevens?"

"That's poetic, but not quite as believable as the hard-core pornography."

"Okay, what I really do is religious/organic gardening manuals, things like *How to Deal Compassionately with Potato Bugs.*"

He stifled a laugh. "Raine, that's enough."

"If I tell you what I really do, you'll have to promise not to laugh."

"Promise."

"I'm a consumer reporter and I'm working on an exposé about how rich people are forced to pay exorbitant prices in Beverly Hills."

The hint of a smile tugged at the edges of his mouth, then unable to contain himself, he broke into laughter.

"You promised," she reminded him.

"You can't expect a reasonable man to keep a promise with a story like that. It's even better than the potato bugs."

"Why is that so hard to believe?"

"Come on, Raine. Unless they're doing something decadent or criminal, nobody cares how the rich squander their millions, least of all the rich themselves. And nobody is holding a gun to their heads, forcing them to shop on Rodeo Drive. Now, enough of that," he said abruptly. "All I've learned from you is how clever you are at manufacturing stories. What is the truth?"

"I'm doing meticulous research on how artists seduce their customers, and I must say your technique is effective."

He felt the frustration welling up inside him again. Damn, couldn't she just once give him a straight answer? Yet it was impossible to sustain any anger at this flaming-haired, mischievous elf. He pulled her on top of him and entwined his fingers in her long hair as he kissed her.

"I don't know that I've ever gone this far to seduce a customer."

"What about that actress with the painting in her bedroom?" she murmured as he thrust his knee between her legs and rubbed gently. She felt electric shocks emanating from the spot.

"Just because the painting was there doesn't necessarily mean I was."

"Who adjusted the spotlights?"

He laughed. "All right, I'll admit it. But it was only once and over a year ago."

"So you seduced her, and after she bought your painting, you never called her again," she said with mock indignation. "Nice guy."

He rolled Raine over on her back and gazed down into her eyes. "You really do think I took you out to get you to buy my litho?"

She struggled to get free, but once again he had her arms pinned down. "Are you going to tell me you never thought I was rich?"

"Those first few minutes when you walked in, but your sister was trying so hard to impress me I sensed something was wrong. I see enough people in there to be able to weed out the genuine from the phonies."

Raine looked up at him suspiciously. "If you knew you couldn't sell me the litho, why did you ask me to lunch, then dinner?"

"Because you intrigued me, and whatever else you were lying about, you meant what you said about my work. You saw in it something few people do, and it made me want to read your poetry, dig inside your soul, and"—his tongue trailed lightly over her teeth— "I wanted to hold you like this in the moonlight."

She wasn't entirely convinced. "Then why did you think I wanted to go out with you?"

"I wasn't sure at first, but I think I know now. I think you also recognized a kindred spirit."

"And you've figured out why I lied to you?"

He gazed at her for a long moment. There was only one answer that made any sense. "Pride. You were afraid if I didn't think you were a buyer, I wouldn't be interested in you. And I'm touched that you would go so far with this house to impress me."

Raine was amazed at how far Ari's imagination had taken him. It confirmed everything Nicole Prasteau had said. The man had a colossal ego. He had even changed everything around to make her into his seducer. Women must really go to extraordinary lengths to get a night in his arms.

The reason he couldn't believe that she was doing an exposé on him was that it didn't fit into his lady killer image of himself. He honestly didn't think a woman could have any other motive than the desire for a date with his precious self. What unmitigated conceit!

He studied her eyes for a long moment. "And I'm beginning to suspect that the reason you keep making up stories about what you do is that you are out of work. Tell me the truth, Raine, do you need a job? If you do, you can come to work for me."

Granted, the sands of Malibu always did have the reputation for being a giant casting couch, but this was outrageous! "Look, I could use a job in a Beverly Hills art gallery, but only to research my article."

"You have it."

She gave him a stunned look. "Ari, I—"

"I wasn't kidding. The young man you met in the gallery the other day was just there temporarily. Starting next week I'll be needing someone to help me."

Unbelievable as it was, he thought her pride was preventing her from admitting she was out of work, and he still wasn't buying her story about the article.

Raine stood up and started back toward the house. Ari Lekas might be the most conceited, unscrupulous art dealer in California, and he might have an ego that would make King Kong shudder, but he was also something of a gallant rogue to offer her a job, thinking she needed the money. "I don't have any art gallery experience," she said uneasily as he draped an arm around her.

"You understand my work and you are articulate. That should be enough to make a sale."

Working there was exactly what Mrs. Grasset had suggested. She even heard Janet's voice yelling, "You ninny, how could you turn it down? Fate drops a precious diamond in your lap and you refuse to pick it up." Janet would remind her that there was no reason to be sentimental about a man just because he was gallant and charming in the moonlight. The most hardened criminals could also be kind and generous people—and expert lovers. And a man who was overcharging customers by five thousand dollars wasn't exactly an eagle scout.

Then again, he might say that he wanted to dig into

her soul, but he could just as easily be covering up for his own lack of judgment. He might very well have taken Janet and her for heiresses, and now that he'd discovered otherwise he was determined to squeeze what little compensation he could from the situation. How did she even know his job offer was on the level and not just a casting-couch moonlit inspiration? She could melt into his arms tonight and tomorrow the job offer would evaporate faster than morning dew.

They walked up the wooden stairs, and as they reached the balcony, he pulled her tightly against him. "Come work for me, Raine."

"If I work for you, then this kind of relationship is out of the question," she said quietly.

"Why?" He looked surprised.

"Because it's never wise to have a personal involvement where you work."

"That's nonsense. My mother and father worked together for years in the hotel. The whole family did."

She tried to draw away from him, but he held her close. "I'll only work for you under the condition that we not become lovers."

"And what if I say I'd rather have you as a lover than an employee?" he murmured as he kissed her neck.

Her body was crying out for him. It would be so easy to give in. What was Janet always saying about men? That if you let them make love to you on the first date, you'll never see them again. She'd always taken that as a warning not so much as to kiss a man on the first date, but now she was thinking it could work to one's advantage. If she made love to Ari tonight, she'd satisfy this gnawing hunger for him and then be rid of him forever. It might not be reasoning Janet was likely to approve of, but at the moment it seemed perfectly logical.

"What will it be, Raine? Lover or employee?"

She drew in her breath, incapable of formulating a rational thought. "You decide."

"I'll expect you at nine o'clock on Monday morning." He let her go and, without looking back, strode through the house and out the front door.

Walking onto the terrace, she gazed up at the stars, then down at the waves breaking on the sand. The little girl in the devil suit was really in a pickle. Not only had she forgotten her lines and tripped on her tail, she'd gotten all tangled up in it. And if she wasn't careful, she'd land bottom first on her little pointed pitchfork.

> Lies like moonlight
> False reflections from the sun
> That blazing, burning star
> That blinds if we stare too long
> Or too hard
> Moonbeams only dazzle
> Or singe
> Never blind or burn

Working the phrases out in her mind, she went into the kitchen and, unable to find any paper, scribbled it on the back of a paper towel and stuffed it into her purse. Another poem. Each time she was with him it happened.

The pounding surf, instead of lulling her to sleep, kept her awake half the night, and she finally found herself wishing he had made the other choice.

Ari turned onto the Pacific Coast Highway and sped back toward town. He kept thinking how beautiful she had looked in the moonlight with her white dress and flowing red hair.

Raine, summer rain. He began to see a painting, narrow shafts of light infused with bright color slanting down like rain pounding the sea. He would design it to capture that ephemeral beauty he had touched on the edge of the Pacific Ocean tonight.

Summer Rain, he'd call it. Odd, it was the first time in months he had thought about painting. How long had it been? Since he'd opened the gallery six months ago and commerce had sapped all his creative energy. Was it all worth it?

He wondered if it had been wise to offer Raine the job. She was wrong if she thought they wouldn't make love. Something elemental was drawing them together, something that cried out for completion. But there was still something dangerously elusive about her he couldn't fathom. Like summer rain you tried to hold in your hands.

## CHAPTER SIX

Monday morning Raine arrived at the gallery promptly at nine, then stood outside and waited fifteen minutes for Ari, who arrived juggling two Styrofoam cups and apologized for being late. "I stopped to pick us up some coffee."

"You don't have a coffee maker?" she asked with surprise.

"Why, no. If I feel like coffee, I send my assistant down the street for a cup."

She groaned inwardly. Even if it was all for the good of *Buyer Beware*, it would take a lot to suppress her indignation at being treated like a servant. "What do you serve your customers?"

"Same thing," he said logically. "If they wanted a cup, I would send you down the street."

She took the Styrofoam cups from him so he could turn the key in the lock. "I can see my first order of business will be to pick you up a coffee maker along with some cups and saucers."

"What's the matter with going down the street?"

"It's a waste of time, for one thing."

"Good exercise for you."

"I prefer jogging."

"Then you can jog down the street for coffee."

"On Rodeo Drive? Designer warm-up suits were

last year's rage. People would spot me right away for a phony and send me packing back to Burbank."

"What's this year's rage?"

"Tennis dresses."

"Then we'll get you a snappy little Saks Fifth Avenue tennis dress you can slip on whenever you have to run down the street for coffee," he remarked dryly.

"It would be more economical for you simply to invest in a coffee maker."

"Next I suppose you'll be suggesting a wet bar."

"Not a bad idea either. But for the time being a coffee maker is a must. You simply can't have people in here to buy a forty-thousand-dollar painting and not offer them a cup of coffee."

"Did you stop to consider that you'd have to be responsible for cleaning the coffee maker?" he reminded her.

"No."

"And the cups and saucers?"

"Well, we certainly can't serve in paper cups," she said reasonably.

As he switched on the lights, she stood enchanted in the midst of the glimmering rainbow paintings. No, this certainly would not be like working in the nursing home. If nothing else, she would enjoy just being here.

"All right, you win," he said. Reaching in his wallet, he pulled out a hundred-dollar bill. "There's a kitchen boutique around the corner. Pick up whatever you think we need."

She took the bill and, after putting it in her purse, sat down at the small desk at the front of the gallery. "Just as soon as I finish my coffee." She popped the lid off the cup and took a sip. "On second thought, this coffee's not bad."

Ari threw up his hands in exasperation and was about to say something when a chubby middle-aged woman wandered in. He greeted her curtly. "May I help you?"

"No thanks," she said quickly, moving away from him. "Just looking."

Raine turned to Ari and whispered, "You should put a sign in the window warning customers not to talk to you until after you've had your morning coffee."

"I'll handle the customers," he growled. "You can open the mail, at least, while you're sipping your coffee."

The woman ran a plump bejeweled hand over one of the paintings, poking at it in places where the paint had been applied thickly. "What're you asking for these things?" she called over to Ari.

"These things," said Ari with slow disdain, "happen to be works of art, and the one you're marking up with fingerprints is thirty-two thousand dollars."

Raine nearly choked on her coffee. In the years she had worked in her father's appliance store, she had dealt with difficult customers, but no matter what they said or did, she knew enough never to be rude to them. "The customer is always right," was their eleventh commandment.

The woman lifted her hand quickly as though it had been burned. "Oh," she mumbled, and sauntered over to another painting.

"I guess you gotta develop a taste for this sort of thing," the woman said in a nasal voice. "It's like all these restaurants now done up with tile walls and tile floors. Makes 'em look like restrooms at Grand Central Station. I know this abstract stuff is all in vogue, but it still looks to me like somebody just threw buckets of paint on a canvas. To me, if you can't tell exactly what it is, it's just cheap junk."

Ari's eyes narrowed dangerously. "Anyone wearing

a rhinestone necklace at nine thirty in the morning could give a new definition to the words 'cheap junk.' "

The woman self-consciously covered up her necklace and, glaring at Ari, stormed out.

"How did you know that was fake?" asked Raine.

"Nothing about that woman was real."

"Do you always treat your customers so courteously?"

"You expect me to stand there in silence while she insults my work?"

"Didn't you ever hear the expression 'The customer is always right'?"

"Any customer who equates my work with Grand Central Station bathrooms is wrong."

"Let me handle the next person who comes in here, let me handle them," she said.

*"You?* After ten minutes' experience in an art gallery sipping coffee you're going to handle a customer?"

"We could pick up a bag lady on Flower Street and she'd do a better job than you just did." Raine stood up and grabbed her purse.

"Quitting already?" he asked.

"No, just going around the corner to get you a coffee maker and some cups. See you in a while." Since he looked capable of throwing something at her, she waltzed out the door quickly.

The coffee makers in the kitchen boutique, like everything else in the Rodeo Drive area, seemed to be cursed with astronomical price tags. After two years at *Buyer Beware* and learning where to find bargains, it was painful to think of spending that much money. Instead, she drove to a discount store on Pico Boulevard and picked up a coffee maker along with six cups and saucers of fine bone china that had evidently been

85

a part of a discontinued or damaged set. There was even a sugar and creamer in the same pattern.

Unlikely as it seemed, Ari's expression had darkened considerably since she'd left. "You were supposed to go around the corner. What happened to you?"

"You thought I'd run off to Burbank with your hundred dollars?"

"It crossed my mind."

"I don't know when was the last time you were in Burbank, but it doesn't go very far there, either. Now, look what I bought you." She unwrapped her finds.

"That's nice," he said, "but what was wrong with that kitchen boutique?"

"What's wrong with everything around here. Overpriced." She handed him fifty dollars and some change.

"You spent fifty dollars on this stuff?" He was appalled.

"You spent that on dinner the other night."

"That was different."

"Why?" she asked.

"Because . . . well, it was. I don't like to spend money on frivolous things."

"I'm glad to know you don't consider me frivolous."

"I may be changing my mind."

She took the coffee maker out of the package and handed him the directions. "Ari, one day you'll thank me for this. It's going to come in very handy."

He gave a weary sigh and went into his back office. Raine smiled to herself. He was probably already regretting his rash act of charity the other night when he hired her. Well, he was in for a surprise if he thought she was going to be a quiet, grateful little mouse. And he was going to be doubly surprised when she started selling.

She remembered the fun of selling appliances in her father's store. Each customer was a challenge, each sale a triumph. But paintings were a drastically different product from appliances. The only people who came into appliance stores were people whose refrigerator or washer had just bitten the dust. And then it was just a matter of convincing them you had the best bargain or the best service.

Getting someone to buy a high-priced painted canvas he didn't need was another story, and she also wondered if she should be selling it at all. Wasn't it unethical to sell products you knew were overpriced? When she had worked undercover in the nursing home, she'd at least been able to give patients some services they ordinarily wouldn't have had. But this was like taking part in a fraud, even though it wasn't exactly like robbing from people who couldn't afford it.

Well, maybe for the time being, anyway, she'd best content herself with being a self-effacing mouse and stay quietly in the background observing.

For all Nicole Prasteau had said about Ari's irresistible charm with women, Raine saw very little evidence of it. He was so sensitive about his work that at the merest hint of an insult, he went on the attack or sat back sullenly and ignored the customers.

Only once, when an elderly woman with a gold-tipped cane came in, did he shed his savage demeanor and act pleasantly. The woman, Raine gathered from the conversation, was an enthusiastic patron who already owned three of his paintings and had donated five others to charitable institutions across the country.

After she'd left, Raine said, "Admit it. Wasn't it

nice to be able to offer her a cup of freshly brewed coffee in a china cup and saucer?"

He grinned at her. "Yes, I'll admit, it was very nice."

"Tomorrow I'll bring in some cookies."

"Raine, I think that's going too far."

"Trust me."

He winked at her. "About as far as I can see you."

Though Raine had planned to turn down any invitation to lunch or dinner, she was still disappointed when he didn't invite her to either.

"See you tomorrow morning," he said cheerfully when she left at five.

Since she had spent most of the day on her feet, the first thing she did when she walked into the apartment was to kick off her shoes, then take a long, leisurely swim in the apartment pool, followed by a soak in the bubbling Jacuzzi while sipping a chilled glass of California chablis. One thing about living in Southern California, she mused, you didn't have to live in Beverly Hills to feel like one of the idle rich.

Janet stopped by on her way home from work and joined her in the Jacuzzi. "What did you learn about your golden Greek god today?"

"I can't figure out how he makes a living, the way he treats his customers. Dad would have had us strung up by our thumbs if we'd talked to people that way."

"Well, somebody's buying his work," Janet noted while adjusting herself in front of the Jacuzzi jet. "If you're talking Rodeo Drive, you're talking a lot of overhead."

She told her about the charming little old lady who came in that afternoon. "There you go," said Janet. "A few sales to people like that at those prices would enable him to get along quite nicely."

"But that woman was a customer long before he

had his gallery and would probably seek him out if he worked in a basement in Cucamonga. What's the sense of having a slick Beverly Hills gallery?"

"Maybe you caught him on a bad day when he didn't have all his Mediterranean charm revved up."

The Jacuzzi turned off and Raine got out to add another fifteen minutes. "Maybe the guy who worked for him before was a good salesman, but I think it's a good case of physicians trying to heal themselves or the saying that the lawyer who represents himself has a fool for a client. I don't think artists can sell their own work. They're too close to it."

The next morning she stopped at a bakery in Burbank that sold inexpensive but rich-looking little tea cookies and arranged them on plate beside the coffee maker.

"Now that I've had a day's experience, will you let me handle some customers?" she asked. Ethical considerations aside, it was gut-wrenching to watch him botch up sales and not do anything about it.

He scrutinized her a moment. "You really think you can handle it?"

"Absolutely."

"I'll be right here if you need to know anything," he said uneasily.

"Ari, I want you to promise me one thing."

"What?" He looked skeptical.

"Whatever I say, don't contradict me."

"I can't promise that, Raine. You might not know what you're talking about."

"Just give me one morning. If I bomb out, you can fire me."

He threw up his hands. "All right. You've got one morning. I'll just sit over here and watch the show."

Nobody came in for the first hour, and Raine was beginning to wonder if anyone would when two women shuffled in dressed in the style Janet sarcastically called "the Turkish tent." A woman had to be six feet tall and built like a telephone pole to pull it off, and these poor ladies weren't a millimeter over five foot two.

Raine approached them with a broad smile. "You ladies are certainly out early this morning."

"It gets so hot later on, we never feel like doing anything but sitting by the pool and sipping vermouth."

"I know what you mean." Raine was looking desperately for something to compliment with sincerity, but it was a hopeless search. "What an unusual ring!" she said to the blonde in red parachute silk. The woman beamed and thrust the ring under Raine's nose. "Do you like it?" The free-form gold ring looked as though it had been extracted from a molar and studded helter-skelter with diamonds and emeralds.

"I've never seen anything like it," said Raine. "Where did you find it?"

"To tell the truth, I designed it myself."

"No kidding."

"It's sort of a hobby of mine. I can never find exactly what I want. This is an anniversary present from my husband. I never let him pick anything out for me. He has absolutely no taste."

"Most men don't," Raine agreed, and stole a glance at Ari, who was suppressing a smile at her comment.

"I can't even let my husband shop for himself," said the other woman. "I'd never take him into an art gallery, for example. He thinks those velvet paintings you get in Tijuana are high art. And if I buy anything, he just wants to know if it's a good investment or not. These are beautiful, by the way."

"Aren't they?" said Raine. "Come over here and

look at this one from this angle, the way the light hits it. Do you see the face?"

"Oh, how fascinating," the woman enthused. "Come on over here, Millie, and look at all those teensy little rainbows in the eyes."

"The exciting thing about Ari Lekas's work is that you can view it from every angle and you always see something different in it. They even change with the time of day."

She moved to another one. "This one is like gazing into a huge cut diamond," said the jewelry designer. "It would look gorgeous in my dining room over the buffet, don't you think, Millie?"

"The blue would pick up the color of your carpeting," Millie agreed.

"How much is it?"

"Twenty-seven thousand dollars," Raine answered.

She shook her head. "A lot of money."

"How much did you pay for that ring?" her friend asked.

"Can I offer you ladies a cup of coffee?" Raine asked them. Both women thought it was a wonderful idea, and Millie even went off her diet and ate a cookie.

"Nice thing about these dresses," she confided to Raine. "They hide a multitude of sins."

And virtues, Raine could have added, but didn't. "Just wander around and make yourselves at home," she said cheerfully.

"Is there any literature on the painter?" asked Millie.

Raine glanced over at Ari, who opened a drawer and handed her a disorganized collection of newspaper articles and certificates from permanent collections. Raine let the women glance through them.

"You don't have any brochures?" asked Millie.

Ari shook his head and Raine said, "Uh, no. We ran out. They're at the printer now."

"I wondered. Usually that's the first thing they give you when you walk into a gallery."

The woman in red came back to the diamond painting and sighed. "I really love this. There's just something about it that makes me feel good."

"That's the only criterion that makes any sense," said Raine. "Some art critic can come along and tell you it's the most beautiful painting in the world, but if you don't feel inside that it's something that's going to brighten your day every time you look at it, then forget it. You might as well put the money into a race horse."

The woman laughed. "My husband's got a few of those too. At least a painting doesn't need a trainer and new shoes every four weeks."

"When you go home this afternoon, look in your dining room and try to imagine it there," suggested Raine, "then come back again and take another look."

"That's a good idea," said the woman.

"In fact, stop by any time and have a cup of coffee and see what new things we have in. Lekas's work moves very fast so I can't promise we'll still have this one, but there'll be others." This was the kind of subtle pressure she used to use in selling TV sets, and she was curious to see how it would work on paintings.

The woman did look worried. "But I do love this one. Would you give me a break if I paid cash?"

"Of course," Raine said quickly. "Ten percent off." Ari's expression tightened, but keeping his promise, he didn't contradict her.

There was some murmuring among the women, then she said, "Will you hold it for me until this afternoon? I'll have to talk it over with my husband, of course, but he always goes along. I've been looking for ages for something wonderful to put over that buffet. I'll be back later this afternoon with a cashier's check for the full amount." She took one last fond look at the painting, then, thanking Raine for the coffee, left.

"You should never give anyone a discount," said Ari, coming toward her.

"You've got to discount a cash sale."

"Why?"

"Because you just do. It's always done in business. And why in the world don't you have a brochure on yourself?"

"The galleries where I've exhibited before always had them done up, but I figured if this was my own gallery I would be there to tell people about myself. I have those certificates and articles if people want proof that I am who I claim to be, but I think the work speaks for itself. People either like it or they don't."

Raine gave an exasperated sigh. "But people also need some reassurance when they're plunking down that kind of money. They may want to take a brochure home and look it over; talk it over with their husbands. I want you to make out a complete list of all your permanent exhibits and the names of some customers who wouldn't mind publicity. I'll excerpt quotes from the articles, and we'll do up a brochure for you."

"Raine—"

"You've got to listen to me, Ari. You are an extraordinary artist, but you obviously don't know beans about running a business. Now let me tell you a little bit about sales technique. The worst thing you can say to people when they come in is 'May I help you?'"

"But that's what everyone in America says."

"My dad would have shot any salesman of his who approached a customer with that."

"Then what do you say to people?"

"Anything that comes to mind that's natural and that can engage them in conversation. The minute you ask if you can help them, they'll immediately clam up and say no, and psychologically you've set up a negative mood for buying."

Ari took a chair and sat down beside her at the desk. "What else?"

She was glad to see that with all his arrogance he realized she was right and was willing to listen to what she had to say.

"Well, you should make your customers feel like they're coming into your home, not your store. That's the reason for the coffee and cookies. It's something you'd do in your own home. And always compliment a customer's taste, pick out something they're wearing, for example. Even if you think it's ghastly, you have to figure they wouldn't be wearing it if they did. You flatter people and they feel good about themselves and you've set up a whole positive mind set toward you for buying."

"Yes, it makes sense." Suddenly he looked at her with understanding. "So that's why you thought I said I liked your poetry."

She flushed. "Well, yes. I just assumed . . ."

He took her hand and kissed the tips of her fingers. "I never flatter people when I don't mean it."

She pulled her hand away awkwardly. "But from now on, when it comes to sales, Ari, you should."

He stood up and looked around the gallery. "It doesn't seem right that you put in a lifetime of hard work to achieve something honest and then you must be dishonest to sell it."

"It's not dishonesty, really." She tried to explain her mother's philosophy of gray lies. "If you're in business, it's just something you use, like a typewriter."

"Business," he said with a scowl. "I always hated anything to do with it."

"Why?"

"Perhaps it was because I saw my father consumed with it. He was always working, thinking of new ways to turn a profit. His children might not have existed for all he cared. We were just pawns to further his business interests. The bride he had picked out for me was the daughter of the man who owned the piece of property next door. He eventually forced my sister into an unhappy marriage with the son."

"I'm surprised you decided to open a gallery."

"In the past I let agents and galleries handle my work, but they were stealing me blind, so I finally took my savings and poured it into this gallery."

"I'll bet you've never even taken a bookkeeping course."

"It's not something they teach you at the Beaux-Arts Academy in Paris," he said with a laugh.

"You do have a bookkeeper, don't you?" she asked with alarm.

"But now that I have you, perhaps I'll fire him."

"No, don't do that. I'm terrible at numbers. Dad always had Janet work the cash register and keep the books while I waited on customers."

"This is the same father who was in, what was it, investments?"

"He was in appliances," she said sheepishly, "as in TVs, refrigerators, stoves, microwave ovens."

Ari took a strand of her hair and twisted it around his fingers. "Will you have dinner with me tonight?"

She moved away from him, busying herself with straightening out the desk. "Don't you remember our agreement? We weren't going to have that kind of relationship."

"Raine, employees and employers do occasionally

dine together without it being the prelude to a passionate night of love. Besides, what makes you so certain I want you?" His black-eyed gaze flickered over her mischievously.

"The way you're looking at me."

"Perhaps you misread my admiration for lust. After the sale you just made I at least owe you a dinner."

"A ten-percent commission would suffice."

He chuckled. "That was the ten percent you gave away for the cash sale. Besides, we have yet to see if the lady of the ring returns with her cashier's check."

The woman did return at four o'clock with a cashier's check and her husband, who gave the painting a squinty-eyed look and a shrug.

As soon as they left, Ari turned around and wrote Raine a check for twenty-seven hundred dollars.

"That's ten percent of the full price," she said.

"So?"

"But you gave the woman a ten-percent cash discount on twenty-seven thousand dollars. My commission should only be ten percent of twenty-four thousand three hundred."

Ari looked embarrassed at his error as he wrote another check. "And we never really discussed whether I was going to be working on salary or commission."

"Why not both?"

How did he manage to stay in business? "Because it wouldn't be fair unless you paid me minimum wage or something. How about if I just work on commission?"

"But weeks can go by without a sale. How will you live?"

She tapped her finger on the check. "This should be enough for a while." She would, of course, have to return the check to him when she left. And yet, somehow, she couldn't get away from the feeling that her ten-percent commission was far more satisfying than any of her paychecks from *Buyer Beware*.

"Now you can't turn me down for dinner," he said as he locked up the gallery. "Your first sale is cause for a celebration."

Perhaps it was.

## CHAPTER SEVEN


"First I want to show you my studio," said Ari as they walked down the street toward the parking lot. "We can have a drink there, then go out to dinner." He paused for a moment. "Unless you're hungry now."

"I can wait. I'd love to see your studio. Where is it?"

"In my house."

She might have known, but it was too late to object now. After one drink, she'd simply insist that they go to dinner.

They drove east on the Sunset past all the movie and record billboards and New Wave boutiques and turned left on Laurel Canyon. Exhaust fumes and smog seemed to evaporate as they started up Wonderland Drive.

"Los Angeles really is an extraordinary city for place names. Just think about it, we've left the glorious hills of Beverly, sped down the Sunset Strip into the canyon of bay laurels to arrive at Wonderland."

He grinned at her. "I love the way your mind works."

"Janet thinks it's a little convoluted."

"Janet, the bubble burster. Don't listen to her."

"I have to, otherwise I'd float up to the sky like a helium balloon and get lost in the stars. Speaking of which, do you know how Hollywood got it's name?"

"How?"

"It was actually supposed to mean Holy Wood. A religious group had settled here, then later the developers came in. Those original settlers are probably turning over in their graves to think of all the glitter and decadence the name Hollywood conjures up now."

"I can remember as a boy thinking how glamorous and exciting Hollywood must be, but now I picture these hills and canyons. There is something still religious and mystical about them."

He pulled his sports car into the driveway of a contemporary house built of burnished wood and brick. There were two tall sycamore trees in front, and in back were hills covered with glowing yellow wild mustard blossoms. "Wonderland," she murmured, feeling a little like the legendary Alice.

"New Yorkers have the most unpleasant things to say about Los Angeles," he said as he opened his front door. "After Paris and New York, I never thought I'd want to live here. Then when I was out for a visit, a friend took me to his house in Benedict Canyon and I was home. Within two months I'd closed up my studio in Soho, bought this house, and opened my gallery in Beverly Hills."

"You don't waste any time mulling over decisions, do you?"

"Not once I've made my mind up to do something."

Inside the furnishings were sparse, a roomy beige couch, a matching chair, a coffee table all in a small grouping near the window looking out over the canyon. The rest of the large living room with the high wood-beamed ceilings was given over to the huge paintings. There were at least four resting on specially constructed easels in various stages of development, others leaning against the walls.

"I like your place," she said with enthusiasm, and walked over to one of the unfinished paintings. "This is beautiful. It looks like you're almost finished with it."

"I stopped work six months ago when I opened the gallery and just haven't been able to get back to it."

"I guess the gallery consumes a lot of time."

"And energy," he said disgustedly. "It takes everything out of you. After a day of looking at my paintings and talking about them the last thing I want to do is work on more of them."

"And before you opened the gallery?"

He looked around nostalgically. "I couldn't wait to get up in the morning to start work. I would roll out of bed, make a cup of coffee, and pick up my brushes, and the next thing I knew hunger was gnawing at my stomach and it was three o'clock in the afternoon."

"That proves the point I was making the other day at lunch," she said. "It's impossible to concentrate on your art if all your energies have to go into another job."

He gave a resigned glance to his unfinished paintings. "Perhaps you're right. But you can't trust other people to sell your work for you. I learned that the hard way."

"What's going to happen when you run out of paintings to sell?" she asked.

He laughed. "Then I'll retire and . . ."

"And do what?"

"I'll take up . . . organic gardening and the cultivation of potato bugs. Who knows?" He opened a bottle of Dom Pérignon with great flourish and they toasted her first sale. "Here's to a long relationship," he said.

Their eyes met and held for a moment. What kind of relationship, she wondered, then reminded herself that it wouldn't last more than the week she needed to research her article. And yet standing there in his home amid his fantasy paintings of light, she suddenly had an aching desire to be with him there forever.

> In a canyon of bay laurels
> we lived in a house of holly
> wood and brick and
> magic light beams
> that linked a chain between
> our souls

"What are you thinking?" he asked. "For a moment you looked so . . . intense."

She smiled and flushed. It was as though she had been caught naked. "Some words that just flashed into my head."

"Tell me."

"In a canyon of bay laurels . . ." She stopped. How could she tell him the next line?

"Go on."

"No."

"Tell me and I'll show you the sketches I did over the weekend."

"That's blackmail!"

"Tell me the rest."

Slowly she repeated the lines, flushing crimson as she said them. When she was through, he took her hand and led her to the drafting table. Her book of poems was open to the inscription she'd written for him. So he hadn't tossed them in the wastebasket. It gave her a tingling feeling to know that a part of her had already been living intimately with him.

She studied the sketches carefully, the slashes of lines. "I hate to admit it, but I don't quite understand how it will look."

"These are rough," he apologized. "The trouble with sketches for a painting is that you're using one medium to illustrate another."

"Not only that," she added, "but with your work there's a kind of fourth dimension with the movement of light and rainbows moving through it. It's hard to imagine in black and white."

"I wish I could show you . . ." He looked around the room, hoping to find something that would give her a general idea of what he was trying to do, but he realized then that he'd never done anything quite like it before. How did you translate the feeling of a warm summer rain on skin that had just been caressed by moonbeams?

"You'll just have to wait until it's finished," he said finally, and glanced at his watch. "We'd better be going to dinner. I wouldn't want to keep you out so late you won't make it to your job on time in the morning."

"How thoughtful of you. My boss is quite an ogre and would fire me if I were as much as two minutes late."

"I shudder to think of you working for such a monster."

"There are some compensations."

"Like what?"

"Well, he takes me to dinner when I've made a good sale."

"What kind of restaurant are you in the mood for tonight?"

Anywhere there was a lot of noise and bright lights. She wasn't going to take the chance on another seductive evening of candlelight and cognac. "How about Mexican food?" she suggested. "I know a wild place in West Hollywood with singing mariachis and pitchers of margaritas, piñatas hanging from the rafters. You'll love it."

If she had wanted to avoid physical contact, she couldn't have picked a better spot. The restaurant was so packed they were forced to sit across from each other at a small table that was hemmed in tightly between others. The mariachis were off key, but the margarita-guzzling customers didn't seem to mind and greeted their favorite songs with loud whoops of appreciation.

"Would you like a margarita?" Ari asked when the waiter came to the table.

"What?"

"Margarita," he said louder.

"Absolutely."

"Guacamole?" he nearly shouted.

"Why not?" Raine was grateful that the constant noise made verbal communication impossible. But to numb the raging feelings warring in her chest as she gazed wordlessly at the golden-haired, dark-eyed man across from her, she downed three margaritas in rapid succession.

"I had no idea what Mexican food was before I came to Los Angeles," said Ari during a brief lull between "El Rancho Grande" and "Las Manānitas."

"Me neither. Now I can't imagine life without enchiladas." Her last words came out slurred. The margaritas added to the Dom Pérignon had been too much. "Have you been to Mexico?" she said, slowly enunciating each word.

"I went to see the pyramids in Yucatán. They're wonderful, then stopped in Acapulco for a few days afterwards."

"Where?" The mariachis were practically at the next table and the bass guitar was thumping loudly in her ear.

"Acapulco."

"Oh." She smiled. "Acapookoo, er, Acapolka." Suddenly her brain wasn't making the necessary connection to her mouth muscles, and at a loss to do anything else, she giggled and took another sip of her margarita. "A taco for your thoughts."

He was thinking that she'd had far too much to drink, and realized he shouldn't have ordered a full pitcher of margaritas. With all the crushed ice and sweet mixer, you had no idea how much tequila you were consuming until it was too late. She was listing dangerously to starboard as she stood up to leave. Ari wrapped a strong arm around her waist as they walked to his car.

"You're in no condition to drive home," he noted.

"But then how'm I going to get home? Oh, damn, it was that last margarita. I knew I shouldn't have had it. Somebody ought to start an initiative to have tequila banned in California. Would you vote for it, Ari?"

"No. I've always been in favor of making it the official state drink. I'm going to drive you home, Raine."

"But how will I get to work in the morning? My boss is an ogre, remember? If I'm a minute late, he'll force Burbank cookies down my throat."

"The ogre will pick you up and drive you to work."

"Out of your way, Burbank is. Just drop me off in the canyon of laurel leaves, and I'll walk over the holly-covered hills into my beautiful downtown Burbank."

"In your condition you could probably fly over the hill if you wanted," he said with a laugh, and pulled her more securely to him. She liked the warm feel of his hard body, and remembering how it had felt to be lying beside him on the sand, she felt a tremor race through her body.

"Got to get home" she murmured.

"I'll get you home."

"Too much trouble. Call me a taxi."

"It takes hours to get a taxi in L.A. By that time I could have you home."

He helped her into the car. "What's the best way to get to Burbank from here?"

"You could go up and over Highland. You take the high road, and I'll take the low road, and I'll be in Burbank before ye . . ." she crooned.

"Wouldn't it be quicker to take Laurel Canyon into North Hollywood and get on the Ventura Freeway."

"You're absolutely right."

"Burbank is next to Glendale, isn't it?"

"Mmmm. Pretty name, Glendale. Glen-dale," she sang out. "All pretty names out thata way. Glendale, Pasadena, Arcadia, and . . . Burbank." She giggled. "Why do I live in the only city in Southern California that sounds as if it was shot out of a howitzer?"

That was the last thing she remembered until waking up some hours later on a couch with a soft pillow under her head and a down comforter tucked around her.

At first panic gripped her. She had no idea where she was and strange lights, like ghosts, seemed to be floating around the room with her. No, not ghosts, they reflected like glass . . . or paintings of glass . . .

Then she remembered Ari and the margaritas. She must have passed out before she could give him directions to her apartment. Maybe Janet was right and she shouldn't be left alone to fend for herself if this was the kind of predicament she got herself into.

Drinking too much was inexcusable. She knew her limit. When she had first begun to date, Janet had sat her down with a bottle of wine and made sure she knew exactly how many glasses would make her feel good and how many more would make her drunk.

Raine buried her face in the pillow. How embarrassing. How could she possibly face Ari in the morning?

She didn't have to wait until morning. Suddenly she was aware of a tall, lean figure standing by one of the paintings watching her.

"Ari?" Her voice was raspy.

As he came toward her, she gradually became aware of his magnificent body with long muscles that tapered down across his hard chest to . . . oh, my God, he was wearing nothing but a pair of boxer shorts. Well, it could be worse, she thought frantically.

It was worse. At that moment she realized that she was stark naked under the comforter.

## *CHAPTER EIGHT*

He sat down on the couch beside her and rested a hand on her forehead. "How are you feeling?"

"A little silly."

"Besides that."

"Like somebody crushed my head under a steam roller."

It was dark, but from the dim light she could see the sinewy outlines of his body, the chiseled angles of his face.

"I guess it's much too late to go home now."

"Much too late," he said softly.

What did he mean by that? Had they already made love?

Feeling embarrassed and vulnerable, she pulled the coverlet more tightly around her. "Did you . . . did we . . . ?"

He smiled. "No, we didn't and I didn't undress you. You fell asleep in the car and I carried you inside and put you on the couch."

"Then how did I get undressed?"

"You woke up and insisted you'd wrinkle your dress if you didn't get it off. You said your sister was always after you for falling asleep in your clothes, and before I knew it, everything was off and you were back under the cover."

"Janet," she said with a sigh. "Even when I'm out

of it, I still hear her voice lecturing me. It's like having my own Jiminy Cricket."

"What's that?"

How did you explain Jiminy Cricket? "He was this little bug who was also a conscience. You see, there was a little wooden boy named Pinocchio who told so many lies his nose grew."

"His *nose* grew if he told a lie?"

She was thankful not to have the same affliction. Hers would be at least twelve inches by now.

"Yes, you see there was this old guy named Geppetto who wanted a child, so he carved himself a wooden boy and—"

"Why didn't he just get married and get his wife pregnant?"

"Because it was a Disney movie and you couldn't have an old geezer running off to singles bars looking for a mate." Ari was not comprehending and she couldn't blame him. "Why don't I give you the plot rundown tomorrow? It's a little complex."

"And you need some rest. You've been asleep for only a couple of hours. I just came in to make sure you hadn't fallen off the couch."

She looked up at him and smiled. "I suppose I'm lucky you were gentlemanly enough not to take advantage of me in my vulnerable state."

He slowly reached under the cover and caressed her, and Raine felt herself grow tense.

"When you and I make love, I want you to remember it."

"*When,* don't you mean *if?*" she managed to whisper.

"When," he repeated, then slowly lifted the cover and slipped under it with her. She was in shock. Every sinewy muscle that touched her body evoked a response. Suddenly she was no longer tired, she was confused and afraid and tingling with longing. She felt the coarse, curling hair of his chest against her breasts, the strong arm under her head, his lips on her forehead.

"Now, go to sleep, my lady of the moonbeams. You have a full day's work ahead of you tomorrow."

Sleep? How could he possibly expect her to sleep with him beside her like that? Astonishment turned to anger as she realized he probably thought she'd be so aroused that she would beg him to make love to her.

"Won't this be a little uncomfortable, the two of us trying to sleep on this narrow couch?" she murmured.

"We can go to my bed."

"And sleep just like this without . . . doing anything."

"You're in no condition to make love."

The man was infuriating! Every nerve in her body was crying out for him, and there he was lying almost naked beside her and not the least interested. He was even dropping off to sleep! She listened with mounting anger as his breathing became slow and even.

When she moved to free her leg from his, he dropped his hand onto her hip, caressing it lightly. "Sleep, Raine."

"What am I, a trained poddle? 'Sleep, Raine; fetch, Raine; roll over, Raine.'" Furious, she sat up and the abrupt movement sent such a stab of pain slicing through her head that she didn't notice the covers had slipped off, exposing her breasts. It did not go unnoticed by Ari, who took the tip of one in his mouth and flicked his tongue over it with soft, sensuous strokes.

She pulled away from him. "Damn it, Ari. You can't do this to me. It isn't fair."

He rubbed the newly moistened nipple with his thumb, enjoying watching it change shape. "Raine, the bedroom is through that door. Go on," he said lazily. "I'll sleep here tonight."

That wasn't what she wanted to hear at all. How could he be so blasé about what he was doing to her? Her head was throbbing with pain while the rest of her was just throbbing.

But she'd be damned if she'd give him the satisfaction of knowing it. "I don't want to kick you out of your own bed," she said flatly. "You won't be comfortable here. Look how your long legs are all scrunched up."

"I'm fine. Go on."

"All right." She rolled over him. "I'm no martyr." Her knees were unsteady as she stood up, but at least she wasn't listing as at the restaurant.

"Good night," she said briskly over her shoulder.

"Raine . . . wait a minute."

She was still embarrassed at being naked, but with his blasé attitude it seemed just retribution to taunt him with it. She pushed back her heavy red hair and wheeled around toward him, her hands on her hips. "What?"

He studied her for a long moment in the half-light of his studio, admiring the subtle planes of her body, the curve of her softly rounded breasts, and the narrow column of her neck. The disheveled red hair fell like a fiery waterfall onto her shoulders.

"Well?" she repeated insolently.

He smiled. "I just wanted to look at you. You're beautiful, Summer Rain." Then, exasperating her further, he closed his eyes and fell asleep.

She switched on the bedroom light briefly to get her bearings. The master bedroom was not very large, but the screened sliding-glass door was open to the back patio and she could hear the crickets and coyotes in concert. Maybe some of Jiminy Cricket's relatives were out there, thousands of little consciences telling her she shouldn't be in this house and in this bed.

The coyotes didn't sound all that far away. She thought about locking the glass doors for protection, but the fragrance of wild lilac wafted in on a breeze. As long as she was living dangerously, she would hope coyotes weren't hungry enough to gnaw through the screens.

The Canyon of laurels was decidedly an untamed place, not unlike the man sleeping in the other room. Well, maybe not so untamed. At least he hadn't ravished her against her will. He hadn't even ravished her with it. The thought of him dropping off to sleep still unnerved her as she climbed in between the cool sheets of the large bed and fluffed a pillow under her aching head.

Strange half-awake thoughts filtered through the haze. Had she once read that the ancient Greek poets chewed laurel leaves for inspiration? And wasn't there a Greek myth about a girl who, when chased by Apollo, was turned into a laurel tree? Maybe Pinocchio had been carved out of laurel wood. And why *hadn't* Geppetto considered marriage if he had wanted a kid so badly? Disney Studios was only a few blocks away in Burbank. Maybe she'd stop by there and ask somebody.

She awoke several times during the night, once to a scurrying sound on the patio. Whatever it was sounded small and furry, not human or coyote. She shut her eyes again, and the next time she awoke it was because of a nightmare. A ferocious ogre had stuffed her mouth and throat with cotton and sent her marching through the Gobi Desert. As she twisted awake, she realized she was dying of thirst. She rolled over to search for the bedside lamp and instead touched a warm, sleeping body.

How long had he been there? Was this some new strategy wherein he thought she would simply roll over into his waiting arms in the morning? She tried to swallow to bring some moisture into her mouth, but it was no use. This was worse than marching through the Gobi Desert.

Trying to be as quiet as possible, she slid toward the edge of the bed. But either Ari wasn't sleeping or he was reacting to a dream. His arm shot out and encircled her waist.

"Where are you off to, Miss Moonbeam?"

"Water," she rasped.

"Don't move."

She looked at his shadowy figure curiously as he took something off the nightstand. "I thought you might be needing it," he said as he handed her a tall glass of cool water.

She gratefully gulped it down. "I think it was the salt on the rim of the margarita glass that finally got to me," she explained. "How long have you been here?"

"A while. You were right. That couch was too short." He took the empty glass and put it on the table. "Would you like some more?"

"No thanks. I guess I'll be getting back to the couch."

He lay back down. "Whatever you prefer, but I won't bother you."

She was too tired to trudge back into the living room and decided that after already spending so many hours with her in bed, he meant what he said. Of course men weren't constructed the same way as women, she reminded herself. When they had too much to drink, they sometimes had mechanical difficulties. Ari probably didn't want to embarrass himself by trying to start something he couldn't finish. The thought was oddly comforting as she slipped back under the covers.

The brief contact with the chill night air made her shiver slightly.

"Cold?" he asked as he adjusted the cover over her.

"I'll be okay in a moment."

"I know," he said as he wrapped himself securely around her, his large hands cupping her breasts. The heat of his long body pressed against her back did more than stave off the cold, and she knew then, beyond a shadow of a doubt, that there were no mechanical problems. At least not now. But he was not caressing her, only holding her for warmth. *Warmth?* She was on fire! If he was hoping she'd give in and attack him, he might be right.

Rapidly losing what was left of her willpower, she snuggled up against him. It was gratifying to hear his breathing grow ragged. Two could play at this game of subtle torture.

He brushed her long hair aside and his lips found her shoulders, her neck.

"I thought you weren't going to bother me," she said slyly.

"Does this bother you?" He ran his hand over her rib cage and circled the soft curve of her belly.

She drew in her breath. "Yes." Everywhere he touched ignited as if by magic. His long fingers slipped between her legs as he began to caress the sensitive inner part of her thighs.

"Do you want me to stop?" he asked as he touched even more intimately.

"Oh . . . Ari . . ." He was rubbing with slow, sensuous strokes.

"Do you want me to stop, Raine?"

"No."

"You're sure?"

"No . . . please . . ."

"Please what?"

"Please . . . don't stop."

He turned her around to face him and their lips met, moist and eager. She trailed a curious hand over the lean hardness of his back, feeling his responsiveness as she scratched lightly over the different textures of his skin, smooth over his hips then roughened with coarse hair on his thighs.

The willpower she had once marveled at was quickly ebbing away. His kisses trailed down her throat, licking the pulse just under the collarbone, then moved down to her breasts. Taking the tips in his mouth, he pulled lightly with his teeth, flicking with his tongue. Raine moaned and arched to him, winding her fingers through his thick golden hair as he went from one breast to the other.

His hard, muscled leg dropped heavily between hers, parting and pressing up between them, rubbing where his hand had been. She cried out softly, then lost herself in the sensations spiraling within her. He was orchestrating her body into a frenzy of sensations, his large hands sweeping over her.

His mouth was moving down from her breasts, his tongue flicking her navel, then moving farther down until she was writhing with so much pleasure she thought she could bear no more. She craved the feel of him inside her, but he withheld the final satisfaction until she cried out for it.

Gazing down at her intently, he made the first hard thrust into her. "Ah, you're beautiful, summer rain," he whispered.

"Ari . . . Ari . . ."

He kissed her lightly, then shoved powerfully into her again and again, and she felt her body moving to his in primitive rhythm. Tears of sheer joy were rolling down her face.

Ari tenderly pushed back her tangled red hair,

kissed her damp forehead, then fell back against the pillows, staring at the ceiling.

Raine suddenly felt alone and uncertain. She ran a tentative hand down his hard chest. "Ari?"

He took her hand and raised the fingers to his lips, kissing them absently. His mind was somewhere else, and she longed to be able to crawl into his brain and to see his thoughts. A few minutes before she was filled with passion and glittering images, and now there was a sad emptiness, a chasm she couldn't cross.

They were two people who had just shared the most intimate of acts, and yet they barely knew each other. She had always vowed never to make love to a man if there was no love between them. But under what category did this fall?

She longed to talk to him about the conflicting feelings whirling around inside her, but he was already breathing evenly and his eyes were closed. Wherever he was, she couldn't intrude. If only she didn't feel so desperately alone.

Ari was not sleeping. He knew she wanted to talk and that as sensitive as she was, she must have felt him draw away. He would have liked to give her all the assurances a woman wants to hear after making love, but he wouldn't lie to her.

The truth was, he was still wary of her. With Nicole he'd had the same gut feelings, but hadn't heeded them. And he had paid dearly. And yet as much as he had cared for Nicole, the feelings for Raine were already stronger. There was something powerful and lyric between them, maybe even love. But there was also something secret and hidden she was keeping from him that warned him to beware.

It had been easy to sleep with Ari when she hadn't known he was there, but now that they had made love, she couldn't find a comfortable position. Every way she turned, she felt cramped. She longed for her own bed where she could sprawl out and pull all the pillows under her head.

How she wished her car were parked outside so that she could whirl up and over Laurel Canyon and into the security of her little Burbank apartment. From there she would call the gallery in the morning and tell Ari she was quitting, and then he would beg her not to leave him. He'd tell her how much he loved her and . . .

Oh, such fantasies! The dreams of poets who chewed too many laurel leaves. Ari didn't love her. She had conveniently fallen asleep naked in his house and he had done what any red-blooded Greek god would do in similar circumstances. And he would have his share of wood nymphs to keep him warm at night when she left.

As the first pale shafts of light shot through the window, casting lavender reflections onto the polished hardwood floor, she slid out of bed quietly, and this time he didn't stir. Standing beside the bed a long moment, she watched him sleep, the beginnings of a beard on his cheeks. His lips were moving, and under the heavy lids his eyes moved restlessly in a dream, the eyebrows coming together in a frown. Then the face softened and he looked very young, boyish.

Hoping the wooden floor wouldn't creak, she walked quietly into the living room/studio. Pastel light was streaming in from the windows like schoolgirl ribbons, illuminating the paintings in its path. She touched them, letting her fingers glide over the smooth and rough textures of paint, following the paths of brush strokes, thinking about Ari's body and the way it had felt when they made love.

Maybe it was only the lingering effects of the margaritas that made her feel so helplessly out of sync.

When she got home she'd load up on protein, B complex vitamins, and calcium. Or maybe it was all just the effects of dehydration.

The kitchen was separated from the larger room by a counter. She wandered in and found a glass in a rack on the sink, rinsed it out, and filled it with water. Though it was refreshing, it did nothing to calm her.

Strong light now flooded through the east windows in golden beams, and several of the paintings began to sparkle. The effect was one of being inside a house made of crystal prisms. She went over to the drawing board and looked again at the sketches he had shown her earlier. She still could make nothing of the slash marks of pencil. Then she saw some words on a sheet of paper that had been discarded along with some early versions of the design.

Summer Rain.

Suddenly she understood. He had been trying to translate his feelings for her into his art—just as she had done with her poems.

Sitting beside one of the paintings, she took a pencil and feverishly wrote:

> No gentle summer rain
> A hurricane of flaming stars
> shooting through the sky.
> Two celestial bodies mesh and twine and slide
> through prisms infused with gleaming shafts
> that whirl and twirl and leap
> in orgies of crystal rainbows
> that moan and burst
> into a thousand shards of kaleidoscopic glass
> and melt onto a soft night wind of wild lilac.
> But like the guitarist
> whose love lasts no longer than the last strains
> of his fugue upon the air

Like the light that plays through his paintings,
ever changing with the dawn

For a moment she considered making a copy for him, then she remembered how he had drawn away from her afterward. She stuffed the poem into her purse and went back to the bedroom.

He stirred when she crawled back into bed beside him, and without opening his eyes, he reached for her, drawing her within the circle of his warmth.

If only there were a way to make it last.

## CHAPTER NINE

She'd been lying in bed trying to sort out the night's events and make some sense of them when Ari's clock radio went off. The night had possessed a misty, surreal quality. Softly out of focus, it had protected her from taking a sharp, analytical look at what she had done. That all quickly disappeared in the harsh light of a morning laden with domestic concerns.

Should she shower here or wait until she was home? Should she make the bed or strip it while he shaved? Make coffee? Make breakfast? The last question was the easiest to answer. There was nothing in the refrigerator and her tender stomach, still rebelling from the margaritas, wouldn't have stood it, anyway. And as to the other questions . . . Well, no. She wasn't his maid, nor his mistress. But what was she?

Thank heaven for small favors, Ari wasn't one of those horrid people who leaped out of bed with a grin pinned on his face, ready to conquer the world. Like her, he numbly pushed himself through a haze, unable to think straight and stumbling into things. It helped ease the awkwardness of the situation. Even if the employer/employee relationship between them were normal, it would be a mess. And with her researching an article for *Buyer Beware,* it was far more complex than even Ari suspected.

There was only one logical solution, and she told

Ari about it as he drove her to Burbank so that she could change clothes for work. "About last night," she began, clearing her throat.

He slipped his hand under her heavy hair and caressed the nape of her neck. "Regrets?"

She nodded. "We really shouldn't have done that."

"It was inevitable."

His easy response annoyed her. "Nothing is inevitable. Things don't just happen. The two of us made the decision to make love and now we are simply going to have to reverse it. We can't work together in the day and sleep together at night."

"What is really bothering you, Raine? Are you afraid it didn't mean anything to me?"

She stared straight ahead without answering him. That did bother her, but she didn't want to admit it, and she wondered if her real motivation in not wanting to continue with the affair was that she'd rather be the first one to say so. "I don't suppose any woman wants to think she's just a member of a chorus," she said tentatively.

"You're not. You're the lead soprano."

"I always sang alto."

"Then you're the lead alto."

"But we can't go on," she said. "Making love changes everything between two people."

"It can change them for the better," he insisted.

"But what if you were to go out for a three-hour lunch with a beautiful actress who wanted to buy one of your paintings? I'd be sitting back at the gallery biting my nails, wondering what you were really up to. And every time we didn't spend the night together I'd wonder what you were doing and with whom."

"That would happen whether we were working together or not," he observed. "It's part of what happens in relationships. The solution is to trust someone."

"The solution, Ari, is to put the relationship back on a platonic level."

"Plato was a countryman of mine, and I don't think he really believed in it either. It's not possible after what's already between us."

"You make it sound as though a thing, like a rhinoceros, were between us!"

Ari laughed. "I think it is more like a magnet."

"Nothing pulled us together but our own free wills, no irresistible outside force. So we should have no problem calling a halt to it."

His dark eyebrows rose. "Then you're really serious about this. It isn't just uncertainty about me?"

"I'm deadly serious."

"Then we will turn back the clock; pretend last night never happened."

He hadn't put up much argument, she noted sadly. So much for being lead alto. She supposed there were plenty more in the chorus to choose from. But she could relax now, knowing she wouldn't have to deal with this added problem when it came to writing the article.

Which reminded her of Janet. Her sister would wring her neck for getting involved with Ari. Raine dreaded telling her. Then it suddenly occurred to her that she was under no obligation to reveal everything to Janet. But how could she not tell her? Never in her life had she withheld anything from her sister. Although both of them at one time or other had kept secrets from their parents, they'd always shared everything with each other.

But why did Janet have to know about this? About anything in her life? She was so used to her older sister's looking over her shoulder like a cricket conscience that even when semi-conscious, she had worried that Janet would criticize her for sleeping in her clothes.

As they walked up the stairs into her apartment, she said, "I'm not much of a housekeeper. Please excuse the mess."

"No need to apologize. I used to tell my father that you cannot be creative and be neat at the same time."

"My sister would be appalled at my bringing someone into my apartment when it looked like this."

"Your sister isn't here and I don't mind, so don't feel guilty. You're never free of her, are you?"

"I've been trying to break away. Getting this apartment was a first step. But sometimes it worries me that I'm only staging a kind of childish rebellion. If I were smart, I'd be listening to her. I'm really lucky to have someone who cares so much about me."

"If she really cared about you, she'd leave you alone to make a few mistakes. Did you ever think that every time she hits you with another well-meaning critique, it makes you feel like a child who can't take care of herself?"

She thought back to last night. "Sometimes I think I am."

"Nonsense. And she's not doing it for your own good. It's for hers. Keeping you thinking of yourself as a child makes her feel invaluable and needed. I realized that with my father. He had to control everyone's lives around him and assured us all it was for our own good. But ultimately, you're the only one who knows what's good for you, and one of these days you're going to have to make your sister understand that or you'll never grow up."

Janet had never seen the charm in this tiny one-room apartment. Raine had rented it more for the balcony that stretched the length of the room and looked down over a quiet park. But Ari seemed to understand instinctively and, opening the sliding glass doors, walked outside.

"This is superb," he said. "And look at your petunias." She had a half-dozen pots of the hot-pink and purple flowers. "I have tried to grow them at home, but the snails get them. Having a balcony is ideal."

"The balcony's my bedroom all summer long. I make up the chaise longue just like a bed."

He grinned at her. "So that you can look up at the stars."

"Yes. Would you like a cup of coffee?"

"No thanks," he said, going back inside.

"Uh, why don't you wait outside while I change?"

"It's not as though we haven't seen each other without clothes," he said logically. "Are you having a sudden attack of modesty?"

"I thought we were going to turn back the clock."

"That's very good in theory."

"In practice too," she said obstinately.

"You would be denying me a great pleasure."

"But we—"

"It has nothing to do with sex," he said. "The artist in me can admire you like a work of art. Last night when you left the studio, you were standing there naked, and I watched the way the moonlight streaming in from the window touched the planes of your body, the way your hair fell on your shoulders. It was a splendid sight."

She felt a tremor pass through her. Damn it, she wanted him again, and despite his denial that it had anything to do with sex, he knew what he was doing. There should be some law against verbal foreplay. All the exquisite details of the night before came flooding back.

He sat down on her daybed and leaned back against

the fluffy cushions, his midnight eyes half closed, watching her. She had to fight not to go to him.

Instead she took a book from a shelf. It was a large art book on French Impressionism. "Here, feast your eyes on this instead."

"Wonderful feast," he said enthusiastically. "I used to go to the Jeu de Paume Museum in Paris once a week when I lived there. That's where all the Impressionist paintings are. The first time I saw them I wanted to cry, they were so beautiful. All those years in Greece when I had been studying light and the tricks it played, suddenly I understood what could be done with it in a painting." He flipped through the pages. "This one by Renoir, for example, is ordinary in a reproduction like this, but the real thing takes your breath away. You feel as though you were standing outside in the park with the sunlight filtering through the trees."

"There's a French Impressionist exhibit down at the County Museum," she said as she took a dress from the closet. "I'm dying to see it."

"Excellent idea. Why don't we go together?"

She gave a weary sigh. "Because, we're not going to see each other outside of work."

"It's hardly out of the question for an art gallery owner to take his employee to see an art exhibit. Consider it an educational experience."

He stood up and walked over to her typewriter. "Have you written any new poetry?" He picked up a sheet of typing paper and she froze.

Were they notes for the article or the poem she had been working on? She flushed as he began to read.

> Lies like moonlight
> False reflections from the sun
> That blazing burning star

That blinds if we stare too long
Or too hard . . .

She grabbed the sheet away from him.
"Why don't you want me to read it?"
"It's not finished, for one thing."
"I let you see the sketches for my next painting."
"That's different. It wasn't so . . . so personal."
"There you're wrong. It will be the most personal work I have ever done."
She suddenly remembered seeing the words "summer rain" on the sketch. They had already woven each other into their creative lives, and now that they'd gone one more step and made love, could it ever be the way it was again?

Raine was thankful it was a busy day in the gallery, because it gave her and Ari little chance to talk, but she was feeling the debilitating effects of a hangover and a night without sleep. It was all she could do after work to get her Mustang over the hill and into Burbank, where, despite a nagging cricket's voice in her inner ear, she soundly fell asleep in her clothes.

Feeling much better the next morning, and much more able to face life, she was just starting to fix breakfast when the telephone rang.

It was Janet. "Where've you been? I tried to get you last night, but there was no answer."

"I heard the phone ringing, but I was asleep and too pooped out to answer it."

"That was only around nine o'clock. Working in an art gallery is that exhausting?"

"Well, no . . ."

"You didn't answer the phone the night before either, or yesterday morning."

"Since when am I obliged to clock in with you every twelve hours?" Raine said with irritation.

"I wasn't checking up, hon, I was worried about you. And I was curious to know how your research was going."

Raine closed her eyes and remembered how Ari's hands had felt caressing her body, the way he looked at her just before he kissed her. She desperately wanted to tell Janet everything, to make a cathartic confession. But another selfish part of her wanted to hoard the memories and to keep them all to herself.

Besides, she wasn't in the mood that morning to have to deal with Janet's disapproval and the lengthy lecture that would follow.

"Raine, please understand, I'm not trying to pry into your life. I know you're trying to be independent with this apartment and all. It's just that sometimes I get so worried about you."

"I know, Janet, and I appreciate it, but . . ." She thought about what Ari had said. "You just have to learn to trust me to take care of myself. Listen, why don't we get together over the weekend and we can talk then. I'm late to work."

"Sure Rainey, take care."

She hung up the phone feeling uneasy. It was difficult enough dealing with deceiving Ari, but keeping something from her sister was like trying to hoodwink the IRS. Eventually they caught up with you.

When she arrived at the gallery, Ari was in excellent spirits. He even let a customer's insult slide off his back. "What's gotten into you today?" she asked.

"I completed the drawings for my new painting last night. Do you know that it is the first new thing I've started since opening this gallery?"

"Congratulations, Ari, that's wonderful." It suddenly struck her that she hadn't written any poetry in a long time either until she met him.

"You're a good influence on me, Raine. I would like to invite you out with me tonight to celebrate, but I guess that's not possible."

She was suddenly wishing she hadn't been so strict about it. "Well, I suppose we could bend the rule a little as long as the boundaries are understood."

"Wonderful. There's an exhibit opening at a gallery down on Rodeo. There will be champagne, of course, and hors d'oeuvres. My friend Kelly's stopping by. We can all go over together."

Raine's heart stopped. "Kelly?"

"She's a sculptor. You'll like her."

Okay, Raine, she said to herself. You're the one who asked for this. You set your own platonic boundaries on this relationship. Now you can't turn around and burn with jealousy because he's made a date with another woman. Clenching her teeth into a smile, she said. "Sounds like fun, but I don't want to tag along with you and . . . Kelly."

"She and I are old friends and there'll be three hundred people there. We'll all have a good time together, and since it's just down the street, you can always take off early if you get bored."

She took a deep breath. "That sounds fine." It didn't at all, but she couldn't back down now.

Kelly stopped by the gallery at six. She was an adorable bubbly little blonde who gave Ari an affectionate kiss and hug that seemed, to Raine's suspicious eyes, indicative of far more than friendship. It was almost enough to make her back out, but she couldn't let him see that it affected her. And Kelly, who was outgoing and friendly, didn't seem to be in the least upset about her "tagging along."

Though the paintings in the gallery were ordinary,

the catered food was ambrosial, complete with ratatouille served as an hors d'oeuvre in endive leaves, Thai satay meat on sticks to dip in peanut sauce, and gigantic strawberries one could dip in chocolate. Raine ate enough to make three dinners and tried not to watch Ari and Kelly, who seemed to know everyone. Even if she wasn't a girl friend, she was close enough to him to make Raine feel like a stranger. While they were deep in conversation with some acquaintances, Raine slipped quietly out the door.

If I'm smart, I'll drive out of Beverly Hills tonight and never look back, she told herself as she drove down Sunset. Since traffic was heavy, she cut over Laurel Canyon. But that was a mistake. All she could think of was the night she'd spent in his Wonderland house.

She'd have to stop working for him. Since they had made love, everything was altered. Every time she saw him with another woman, even if it was a friend like Kelly, she would die a little. It was futile trying to research her article there; best to quit now before she got involved any deeper.

The following morning she was just about to dial the gallery number and tell Ari she was quitting when the phone rang. It was Bart McCracken.

"So, how are you doing?"

"All right," she said uneasily. "How are things down there?"

"The same. Got anything new on the gallery business?"

"It's not as if people were trampling him under in a stampede to buy the stuff," she said. "A lot of tourists mill through those stores. He's only made one sale in the four days I've worked there, and I suspect that might be it for the week—even the month." She thought it expedient not to mention that she'd been the one to make the sale.

"Yeah, but at those prices, all he has to do is sell one a month."

"Don't forget that's a high-rent district," she told McCracken. "His overhead is astronomical. I don't think I'm going to get much from working there. On the other hand, I've done some price comparisons of things like coffee makers and I think if I pursued that angle—"

"Nah, coffee makers make for dull copy. Stick with this gallery for a while. It's glitzier. It may take some time to get any solid information out of this guy. He's got to build up some trust in you."

"But, McCracken . . ."

"Give it at least another week. Grasset loves this art gallery story. Nearly split her seams when she found out you managed to land yourself a job there. She's even talking about featuring it on the cover. I haven't seen her so enthusiastic since we got the scoop on those flammable kiddie pajamas."

"Okay," she said with a sigh. "Just one more week, but I can't promise I'll be able to get you anything."

"Do the best you can."

McCracken's words echoed in her mind when she walked into the gallery that morning and saw Ari standing amidst his paintings sipping coffee. The best she could possibly do was to keep herself from falling in love with him. And for that, she feared, it was already too late.

## CHAPTER TEN

Ari turned his dark eyes on her. "You're late."

"That's because I was sitting by the telephone this morning contemplating quitting."

Her response temporarily took him off guard. "What made you change your mind?"

"I didn't know what you'd do without me."

He laughed. "Damn right. I've decided to take you up on one of your suggestions."

"Which one?" said Raine as she poured herself a cup of coffee. "No. Let me guess. You've decided to be pleasant to your customers?"

He gave her an indulgent smile. "No, I'll leave being pleasant up to you. You're so much better at it than I. Especially this morning."

She recognized his comment for the dig it was, since she was obviously not in the best humor. Coming to the realization that you were falling in love with someone was ominous business. She tried to force a smile. "Tell me, which of my brilliant suggestions have you decided to act upon?"

"Remember how you said I should have a brochure? Well, you're absolutely right. But besides a brochure, I want to do a book. Last night at the opening I ran into an old friend, the photographer who took the pictures of the painting in the desert. He's coming over this morning, and we're going to talk about his photographing everything."

"It's a wonderful idea," she said excitedly.

He put his coffee down, placed his large hands on her arms, and gazed intently into her eyes. "Will you help me with it, Raine?"

She trembled at his touch. He was so close and she wanted him so badly. "Of course I'll help you. Do you want me to write the biography?"

"Yes, but I want you to do something more, something that will make it unusual, not just another art book to put on the coffee table." His dark eyes were sparkling with reflected light from his paintings. "Raine, I want you to write poetry for the book."

She gazed up at him with astonishment. "I'm not quite sure I understand."

"Then I'll explain it better. On one page will be a photograph of a painting or lithograph and on the opposite one, a Raine Walken poem."

She looked around the room and felt a wave of panic. "You want me to write a new poem about each of these paintings?"

"If one inspires you, yes. But we can use some of the poems you've already written. They don't have to be specifically about the artwork. I reread your poems after I got home last night. The way you write about light and emotions—you capture in words what I've been trying to say with my art. Putting it all together in a book would be the perfect combination."

"I don't know, Ari." She broke away from him and sat down at the desk.

"What don't you know?"

"It's such an awesome task, and to think my poems would be printed in a huge book. I was intimidated enough to see them in a little pamphlet. A book with your paintings is a wonderful idea, but using my poems . . ."

She couldn't finish her sentence because a huge bear of a man with a bushy black beard walked in the door and yelled *"Hóla amigos!"*

"Raine, meet the photographer I was telling you about. Diego Alvarez, meet Raine Walken."

Diego was beside her in two giant strides. "So you're the poet. Ari let me read some of your stuff last night. It's very good. What do you think of doing the book?"

She felt uneasy about Ari showing him her poems. It was as though he'd done a nude painting of her and then turned around and displayed it to all his buddies. But once over the initial shock, she was flattered he'd wanted one of his friends to read it, and even more that he wanted to include her poems in a book about his work.

Since there were few customers in the gallery, the three of them walked around the room, talking about how to photograph the work to best advantage. It was decided that they would shoot all of them outdoors in natural light, even though it would be harder to control the reflections. The uniqueness of the book would be how the paintings interacted with different environments juxtaposed with poetry.

"I'm excited about this," said Diego. "Let's get going on it. What are you guys up to Sunday?"

"I'm free," said Ari. "What about you, Raine?"

"Do you really think I should go along? I don't know anything about photography."

"But you should be there to take down your thoughts," said Ari. "Like a sketchpad, note your impressions. You may want to use them for the poetry."

There was also an ethical concern she couldn't tell him. How could she write an exposé on his gallery and at the same time write poetry for his book? She would have to make a choice, and it wasn't a difficult one. This was the most exciting writing assignment she'd ever had in her life. Ever since she'd met Ari Lekas she had been trying to put her feelings about him and his work into words. She had already been doing it in sporadic inspired gusts of creativity. But now she would be forced to think poetically for a major project. It was a good test to see if she really had the makings of a poet. Either she would crumble or come out with the best work of her life.

She would simply call Bart McCracken and tell him she was quitting *Buyer Beware*. Janet would be upset, of course, but she knew Raine had never been that happy doing articles on subjects like why you couldn't find USDA choice meats in the major supermarkets. This was her life, and she couldn't let this opportunity slip by her.

Diego left after a few minutes, but his heady exuberance continued to permeate the gallery. She and Ari exchanged a laughing glance, then he hugged her. "It is exciting, isn't it?"

"Yes," she admitted. "I just hope I can do it." His arms around her felt much too good, and she broke away from him reluctantly.

"You didn't stay very long at the opening last night," he remarked.

"I saw the paintings, ate enough food to make up for dinner, and decided there was no more reason to stay."

"What did you think of the paintings?"

"Mediocre to dull."

"I agree," he said. "Kelly thought so too. She was ready to leave after five minutes."

Raine felt a twinge in her chest. It didn't matter that

Kelly was just a friend. "How long did you stay?" she asked, trying not to let her jealousy show.

"Diego and I left about an hour after you did."

"What happened to Kelly?"

"She met some guy there and took off with him."

Suddenly curious, Raine asked, "Would it have bothered you if I had met a man there and left with him?"

"I'll be honest," he said, toying with a strand of her hair. "I couldn't promise I wouldn't rip somebody to shreds if I saw him leave with you."

"Even though you and I are only . . . friends?"

"That was a rule you imposed and I am going along with it, but it doesn't stop what I feel inside."

That night Janet stopped by her apartment. "Raine," she said, picking up some shoes off the floor, "why don't you put them back on the shelf where they belong?"

"Because the first thing I want to do when I come inside is kick off my shoes."

"But it's dangerous. Somebody's going to trip over them."

Raine started to bristle, then realized Janet was right. But it was a matter of principle. "Janet, leave them where they are."

"Don't be childish."

"When I come into your apartment, I don't go around picking things up off your floor, do I?"

"I don't leave things on my floor for people to trip over."

This was a no-win argument, but Raine felt she had to make her point. "Janet, you and I both know the shoes are there, so we won't trip on them. I may put them away later. Then again, I may leave them there so they'll be the last thing I put on when I go off to work tomorrow."

Janet heaved a sigh and dropped the shoes back on the floor. "How's it going at the gallery?"

"Very good."

"What have you learned?"

"That it's time for me to get out of consumer reporting."

Janet's mouth fell open. "What do you mean by *that?*"

"Ari wants me to do a book with him," she said excitedly. "It will have photographs of his paintings on one side and my poems on the other."

Janet was obviously not sharing her enthusiasm. She took her hand and led her over to the couch. "Let's sit down and talk about this," she said carefully. "You mean you're going to quit *Buyer Beware?*"

"That's right," Raine said with a smile.

"Have you told McCracken yet?"

"No. I'm going to call him tomorrow."

Janet began to breathe easier. "At least I arrived in the knick of time! Now, what brought all this on? Oh, no, I can see it already. That look. You've fallen for this guy."

"Well, I . . ."

Janet's eyes rolled to heaven. "Rainey, dear Rainey."

"Don't start 'dear Rainey-ing' me. I'm old enough to make my own decisions about my own life."

"Age has nothing to do with it. You'll still be doing crazy things when you're seventy. Starry eyes is one of those incurable, progressive diseases. You had more common sense at seven than you have now."

Raine stood up and walked across the room to put some distance between her and Janet. "What in the world is wrong in my doing a book with Ari?"

"Do you have a contract with him?"

"No, but I'm an employee in his gallery."

"And you have no employment contract either."

"He's perfectly legit," she said defensively. "In fact he's already given me a commission check for a painting I sold."

Janet was aghast. "You actually sold one of his overpriced paintings?"

"I was going to give him back the money when I quit to finish the article."

"But not now."

"Well, once I quit *Buyer Beware,* I'll need to earn a living somehow."

Janet glared at her. "Taking money from someone who's overcharging is like stealing, Raine. It doesn't make any difference if the people can afford it or not. It's just not ethical."

"But everyone's charging those prices on Rodeo Drive," said Raine.

"Remember what Mom used to tell us? She didn't care if we said every kid on the block was cutting classes. That didn't make it right."

Nervously, Raine ran a hand through her hair. "But you know that I've always wanted to do something with my poetry, and a chance like this doesn't come knocking on the door every day."

"I think it's more than poetry that's influencing you," said Janet wisely. "What have you and this handsome Greek been up to?"

"Well, we went out the other night and—"

"And *what?*"

"I don't have to tell you every detail!"

"Raine, you were researching an article on this man. That breaks every code of journalistic ethics in the books! Now you're going to throw away a good solid career in consumer reporting to do something flighty like writing poetry for some art book."

"It's not just some art book," Raine said defensively. "It could be a very important statement about Ari's work . . . and mine."

"Does he even have a commitment from a publisher?"

"Well, not yet, but I'm sure when we have the photographs and poetry together . . ."

Janet groaned. "I'm going to have a heart attack. Do you know what kind of advances they give for that kind of book. Maybe five thousand dollars if you're lucky. So, let's say you and Ari split that, if he intends to give you half. Have you even discussed percentages with him?"

"Of course not. We're still talking about the concepts."

"Concepts?" Janet sighed loudly. "Please, please, Rainey, don't give McCracken notice right away. Take a week to think it over rationally. You know how hard it is to find a job in this town as a writer. Working in an art gallery may be fun, but it's a waste of your education and talent. And this business about doing a book with your poetry and his paintings sounds very fishy to me. Before you write one word, I want you to sit down with a literary attorney and set up the exact terms of that partnership."

"All right." Raine sighed. "I'll put off a decision until Monday."

"And there's another consideration," said Janet.

Raine steeled herself for another bubble burst. "What's that?"

"If you do decide to work for Ari, what are you going to tell him about *Buyer Beware?*"

"I . . . hadn't thought about it."

"You mean, you thought you'd just neglect telling

him that the reason you accepted his job offer in the first place was to secretly exploit him for an exposé."

"Well, I wouldn't be doing the exposé, so why tell him?" Janet raised her eyebrows and Raine recanted. "Okay, maybe you're right. I should be honest with him, but it seems to me that falls in the gray area of lies."

"Of self-serving lies," Janet pointed out. "You're worried that if you tell him the truth, he'll drop you like a hot potato. And I wouldn't blame him."

"I don't know," she said defensively. "He could turn out to be very understanding. Maybe he wouldn't even mind if I continued working for *Buyer Beware* and still did the poetry for the book."

Janet looked at her askance. "I think it's wishful thinking, but who knows? That would be an excellent solution. You'd still have the security of your job at *Buyer Beware*, and you could do your poetry on the side."

Raine did think hard about it the rest of the week. Logic was all on Janet's side. Though she had never been wild about consumer reporting, at least it was writing, and unlike advertising copy, it did some good. Then again, there was nothing demeaning about working in an art gallery, and if she made many more commissions like the last, it could be lucrative.

What she finally decided was to take a chance. Her conscience wouldn't allow her to continue working for Ari without telling him the truth about *Buyer Beware*. She'd just have to hope he would be understanding enough to keep her on. But getting up the nerve to tell him was another thing, and she kept putting it off until late Saturday afternoon just as they were about to close.

"Ari, can we talk a minute?" she said hesitantly.

"How about if we go out for a drink and talk?" Just

then the telephone rang, and at the same moment an Oriental couple walked into the gallery. "I'll get the phone," said Ari. "Why don't you take care of these people?"

Raine was glad for the new delay, even if it only put off the confession for a few minutes. She graciously invited the people in to walk around.

It was evident they were mesmerized by the lithograph she loved. "I love all the work here, but this one is a special favorite," she told them. "It's the strangest thing. It seems to change at different hours of the day, even one day to the next. Come over here and look at it from this angle. You see the way all the prisms converge?"

The couple stepped back from it and talked rapidly in their language. It was obvious they appreciated the work. After a week of uninterested customers, that, at least, was gratifying.

"How much is it?" the man asked finally.

She told them and he blinked several times. "Do you not think ten thousand dollars is very high?" he asked Raine.

Raine told them about the permanent collections where Ari was represented. "This is an extraordinary work," she said. "And it is an edition limited to only six. Of course, if you are really interested, you could make an offer."

Ari, who had just hung up the phone, winced when he heard what Raine said.

The couple discussed it between themselves and walked up close to it again.

"It could be crated safely for shipping to Tokyo?"

"Absolutely," she said. "Lekas paintings have been shipped all over the world."

There was some more conferring.

"I would like to make an offer of eight thousand dollars."

Ari came to life and walked over to them. "You know that the value will double the minute you buy it," he said.

"Double, how?" asked the man.

"Because I do such limited editions of lithographs, the minute one sells, the price always doubles."

"How many more are there left?" he asked.

"Only one."

Although Raine talked up the work enthusiastically because she loved it, she had never used the double-your-money pitch, and it made her uncomfortable to hear Ari using it. As soon as she came to work for him full-time, she'd talk to him about it. Maybe she'd even mention it tonight when she told him about *Buyer Beware*.

"Eighty-five hundred," said the man. "That is all I'll pay."

"Ninety-five," said Ari.

"Ninety," the man came back. It was obvious both men were enjoying the bargaining process.

Ari shook his hand. "You have a lithograph."

As Raine made out the papers and took down the shipping information, she felt a strange letdown, as though she were making out adoption papers for a favorite child.

After the couple left, Ari whirled her around the gallery. "You're wonderful, Raine! This deserves more than a mere drink. It calls for champagne."

"I don't feel much like celebrating," she said quietly. "That was the one I wanted for myself. I'm going to miss it."

"But there is still one more. You can buy that one."

"Sure, Ari. Especially now that the price is eighteen thousand."

"I wouldn't charge you that much. Besides, you just made a nice commission. You can use it as your down payment."

"I don't deserve the commission," she said. "You're really the one who concluded the sale."

"But it was what you said about the work that made those people want to buy it."

"I was just confirming what they already knew. Ari, are you really going to double the price on the last one?"

"Actually, I may not sell it at all," he said lightly. "How could I sell a piece that inspires your poetry?"

He was evading the question, and though she wanted to get a direct answer, she first had to address the matter of *Buyer Beware*. Okay, Raine, she said to herself. Out with it. She lifted her chin and took a deep breath. Why was the truth so hard to get out?

"Hey, how about that champagne?" he said.

"Great idea," she responded quickly, hating herself for being such a coward. But after a glass of champagne, she vowed, she'd tell him.

"I know just the place. It is a restaurant where all they serve is caviar and champagne."

"Only in Beverly Hills," she said, and laughed.

Ari was in excellent spirits as they walked into the plush interior of the champagne and caviar restaurant. He steered her to a dark booth toward the back and slid around to be close to her.

"Here's to our collaboration," he said, lifting his glass to her in a toast.

How would she ever broach the subject of her deception now? The only thing was to let him have another glass of champagne while she sipped hers intermittently. She wasn't making that mistake again. The last time she had had too much to drink, she had ended up in his bed. And seeing him in the darkened light of the room, his black eyes looking sultry and mysterious, she was already having a difficult time concentrating on what she was going to tell him.

Ari could sense that something was on her mind. He hoped it was a change of heart about their relationship, but he was never really sure when she got that look in her eyes. His thoughts drifted to Nicole and the telephone call he had received from her just as they were closing. Why had she suddenly decided to make contact again after all this time? Was she having a change of heart about trying to ruin his reputation? He'd know soon enough what was on her vindictive little mind. She was coming into the gallery Monday morning. That would mean Raine would meet her too. Perhaps he'd even tell Raine about Nicole tonight so she'd have some preparation for meeting her on Monday.

Suddenly they heard a booming voice call out, "Ari! Raine!"

Diego was coming toward them. He was with a tall, willowy woman he introduced as a fashion model. They'd just finished shooting a Neiman-Marcus ad.

Ari invited him to join them, and the four of them had some more champagne, then decided they were hungry. Diego insisted on taking them all to dinner at a new Italian restaurant that had just opened up on Camden and Wilshire.

Raine was going to decline, but she was hungry and decided to go along. By the time they finished the seven-course meal, it was close to midnight.

Ari walked her to her car in the nearly deserted parking lot. Whatever else Rodeo Drive might be, it wasn't a haven for late-night carousers. Even on Saturday night sidewalks rolled up after midnight.

She stood for a moment looking at him. There really

was no use in denying it; she did love him. Every nerve in her body ached for him.

As if sensing her feelings, he pulled her close and touched his lips lightly to hers. She came alive and wrapped her arms around his strong back, returning his kiss with passion.

"Come home with me tonight, Raine."

She disengaged herself. "Ari, I . . ." She couldn't let that happen again before she made a full confession about her work for *Buyer Beware,* and she couldn't talk about something like that in a parking lot. Nor could she wait until she was in his bed.

"Don't fight it, Raine. We need each other."

"We've got to give it time," she said uneasily as she unlocked her car door.

"We've given it time and we both know how we feel."

"Tomorrow after the shoot, let's talk about it," she said.

She had bought a little more time, but when that time was up, she'd still have to face him with the truth, and it wouldn't be any easier.

It was a typical May day in Southern California. It was overcast Sunday morning with low-hanging clouds that would probably burn off later in the day. Raine drove up Wonderland at six A.M. with all the windows down, breathing in the fresh smells of chaparral in Laurel Canyon.

When she pulled up in front of Ari's house, he and Diego were already carefully loading paintings into Diego's van. By six thirty they were stopping at McDonald's for Egg McMuffins and had filled a thermos with coffee and packed a cooler with soft drinks, beer, and fresh fruit.

Diego wanted to photograph them first in the desert. "On the way out we can set up some shots on Vasquez Rocks, then on the outskirts of Palmdale we'll take some pictures among the Joshua trees."

"What a shame it's so overcast," noted Raine.

"Best time to shoot," he said. "There's a nice diffuse light, and we'll get some great shots of clouds in the background."

Raine was fascinated by the huge, looming gray boulders of Vasquez Rocks, named after the bandit who made it his hideout while terrorizing the tiny pueblo of Los Angeles in the last century.

As Diego walked around the rocks snapping pictures of the paintings and readjusting the white umbrellas that deflected light onto them, she found herself watching Ari. He was sitting on the rocks, his dark eyes intently studying nature's own handiwork. Taking out her notebook, she wrote:

> Like a statue, he sits
> On a rock
> Comparing Her work
> to his own
> Is there some disdain in his cool eye?
> He who creates illusions in light
> While Nature is content to cast them
> in stone.

She looked up and saw Ari grinning at her and felt a rush of pleasure. At moments like that she was conscious of some overpowering force drawing them together.

By the time they reached the Palmdale desert the sun was high and the sky was a bright cobalt-blue. They broke out the first of the cold soft drinks as they set up the paintings and equipment. She was carefully brushing some sand off one of them when Ari said, "Diego, come here."

She looked up to see what had drawn his attention. "No," he told her, "stay just as you were, leaning over the painting. Diego, look at the way her red hair tumbles down over it with the Joshua trees in the distance. Do you think you can get that? It's one of the most beautiful sights I've ever seen."

Raine nearly found herself as a model, but very quickly declined to be in more than a few shots. "It's the paintings you want to showcase," she pointed out. "A woman in the picture will only draw attention away."

It was an hour and a half drive to the beach just north of Zuma, where Diego wanted to catch the sunset. By the time they arrived, they were all exhausted, but a scarlet-streaked sky made the trip worthwhile. The rainbow paintings set against it looked spectacular. Exhausted after being up so early, they stopped at Alice's Restaurant in Malibu for a seafood dinner, then drove back to Ari's house and unloaded the paintings.

"I know a lab that will do up the transparencies in a few days," said Diego. "As soon as I have them, I'll stop by the studio so we can all take a look. Depending on what we have, it may require another day or two of shooting."

Suddenly Raine found herself alone with Ari. It was time to tell him about *Buyer Beware*. She even had an article with her by-line stuffed into her purse in case he still refused to believe her.

"Ari," she began.

He smiled at her. "It was a good day, wasn't it?"

"A wonderful day," she agreed, "but tiring."

He came toward her and ran his cool fingers over

her cheek. "Look at you. Your face matches your hair," he teased. "You should have worn a hat."

"Somehow I can never get myself to wear one. They make your head so hot."

"My hotheaded poet."

"Ari, we have to talk."

He slipped an arm around her shoulders and led her to his couch. She couldn't help remembering the other time she had fallen asleep there and what had followed.

"What is it, my pretty summer rain?" She was melting into his dark-eyed gaze. He took her face in his hands. "I'll make it easy for you. Just tell me you love me a little."

"I think," she said breathlessly, "I love you more than that."

His large hands swept down over her body as the kiss deepened.

The confession could wait. It would have to. She could not utter another word.

## CHAPTER ELEVEN

Before she knew it she was back in his bedroom, sprawled across his large bed. He was tenderly removing her clothes, while feathering warm, tingling kisses down her body, the magic igniting nerve endings and making her tremble with anticipation.

When they had made love before, it had been in a sleepy haze, but now she was wide awake and every sensation seemed to multiply in such agonizing intensity that she wasn't sure how much she could bear.

They melded into a hundred different configurations, as though the two of them were sculpting light beams with their bodies.

His lips moved down from her breasts, his tongue lingering at her navel. Then he pushed her legs apart, and he kissed and caressed the soft insides of her thighs, his mouth moving slowly, tantalizingly closer to the center of her desire.

"Oh, Ari . . ." she moaned as his mouth and fingers worked their shattering magic. Her head twisted back onto the pillows as she felt herself arching to him. It was as though she were being wrapped in neon ribbons of electric blue and red.

Feeling her shuddering quakes of passion, he wrapped her legs around his waist and thrust inside her.

Grabbing his strong shoulders, she pulled herself up

to face him. His heavy-lidded dark eyes were fiery and his lips slightly parted. He took a deep breath through his teeth, then thrust deeply into her again, drawing out slowly.

"Do you like that, my beautiful summer rain?" he said hoarsely.

"I love it . . . oh . . . love you, Ari."

He smiled as he tightened his long fingers around her hips and changed the angle to give her more pleasure.

"You're my love, my life, my inspiration, my beautiful summer rain."

The slow circling dance became frenzied and wild, her body wanton with unbridled passion that seemed to inflame him even more. The pleasure increased again and again, until she was sure she could stand no more, until it broke into a searing scarlet wave of delirious spasms. As the tears streamed down her face, he tenderly kissed them from her cheeks.

When at last she felt some sense of reality return, Ari was blowing cooling gusts over her damp body. Pushing her hair off her forehead, he said, "All week long I've been thinking how much I wanted to make love to you. It was hell to be near you and know that I couldn't have you. To hell with Plato and his misbegotten ideas. We can't let that happen again."

She smiled lazily up at him. "It was the same for me, but I've been fighting it."

"No more fighting, my love. It is dishonest to love someone and pretend that you don't. Let's not ever be dishonest with each other."

Integrity. He had to bring it up, she thought dismally. But how could she tell him about *Buyer Beware* now, while they were in each other's arms. You're a coward, Raine Walken, an absolute coward!

Watching her expression, Ari once again had the

feeling she was keeping something from him. Was it that she had another lover? The guitarist she wrote those poems about? He had to know.

Kissing her forehead, he said, "Tell me about the guitarist you loved."

"Ari!"

"You don't want to talk about him?"

"I don't ever want to think about him again. Why should you even care about him?"

"I want to know everything about you."

"I told you all there was to know about him," she said.

"Describe him."

"He wasn't very good-looking," she began reluctantly, "rather thin with light brown hair and eyes. I went to one of his recitals at UCLA with a friend who knew him and there was a reception afterward. We began dating, and I thought I was in love with him, but I don't think so now."

"Why not?"

"Because it wasn't the same as what I feel for you. The turbulence, the passion—even if I'm standing in the same room with you, I'm consumed with it."

"You must have been an inspiration to his music."

She smiled sadly and ran the tips of her fingers across his cheek. "I was never an integral part of his work, only peripheral to it, while he was the center of my creative world. It was a lopsided love at best. But it's been over for a long time. Will you tell me about the women you've loved?"

He leaned back against the pillows and clasped his hands behind his head. He didn't really want to tell her about them, especially Nicole Prasteau, but he had brought up the subject and she might as well know. Besides, she'd meet Nicole soon enough. "There were two women."

"Both at the same time?" she gasped.

He chuckled and pulled her head playfully onto his chest. "No, at different times. One in Paris and one in New York."

Curiosity now had Raine in its grip. "Tell me about the girl in Paris. What did she look like?"

"She had hair that was so blond it was almost white, and large blue eyes. I'd never met such a free spirit. She would jump into fountains and climb up on statues. I never knew what she was going to do next."

"Aha! So unpredictability excites you," said Raine, nibbling on his ear. "I'll have to find a fountain to jump into. There aren't that many in Los Angeles. Oh, wait a minute, there's the fountain at the corner of Santa Monica and Wilshire across from the Beverly Hilton. I'll jump in that some night if you'd like."

He pulled her close. "I have matured considerably since my student days."

"Cartwheels down Rodeo Drive at high noon on Monday?"

He kissed the tip of her nose. "It would be a splendid sight."

"Or I could pogo stick up the center line on Wilshire at midnight."

"You would really do that?"

She sighed. "No, the truth is, I have a soaring imagination, but I'm too chicken to do anything really bizarre. Tell me about her."

"Her name was—"

Raine put a hand over his lips. "I don't want to know names."

"Why not?"

"Somehow that would make her a real person."

"But she was a real person."

"To you, but not to me. If you just talk about the girl in Paris or the girl in London or the girl in the

Laundromat, they're shadowy ideas, not real people. The minute you started to say her name I felt a stab of jealousy."

"And not until then?"

"Well, a little before."

"You don't want to hear any more?"

"I do," Raine protested.

"I've never had a girl in a Laundromat."

"Thank God. But you must tell me everything else. I know exactly how you feel about wanting to know everything. I want to see baby pictures of you and pictures of your dog and the house where you lived in Mykonos."

"We'll go there on a vacation. How's that?"

Her eyes grew wide. "The Greek islands. It's out of a dream."

"I'd like you to meet my family. I have some pictures," he added. "Would you like to see them?"

He started to get up, but she held his arm. "Don't move. I'd love to see them, but first why don't you finish telling me about the girl in Paris."

He closed his eyes. "When she was a little girl, her mother took her to see the opera *La Bohème,* and she'd always fancied herself a languishing Mimi with an artist starving in a Parisian garret. She once even told me she loved me because I was, in her words, bohemian and beautiful."

Raine ran her hand over his hard chest. "Not a bad description."

"It was a very difficult time for me financially," he continued. "There's an American expression—trying to sell ice to the Eskimos. Well, that's like trying to sell art in Paris. She thought I would have better success in New York, so we moved there and got married. But the art market is just as difficult there, and she was getting tired of playing Mimi. On the Left Bank our life had seemed romantic, but in New York her mother used to visit and burst into tears at the way her daughter lived. So she filed for divorce and married a stock broker who commuted into the city every day from Darien, Connecticut."

"It doesn't sound as if you were very upset about it."

"Not now, but at that time I was. I never realized how much I had come to depend on her love. Whenever I had doubts about my work, she'd always been there to keep me going."

"You, Mr. Humility, once had doubts about your work?" she teased. "I find that hard to believe."

"When you are working fifteen hours a day and your paintings are hardly selling, you can't help but harbor some doubts. And after she left me, I couldn't do anything for two months. I would spend hours walking around the city thinking about her and wondering if perhaps my father had been right all along.

"Then I met a woman who began to make me feel good about my work again. She even introduced me to a dealer, who began to handle my paintings. Perhaps it was on the rebound, but she was very beautiful and charming and I found myself falling in love with her."

"And what happened there?"

His eyes narrowed. "I gave her many of my paintings and lithographs as gifts and found out that she was turning around and selling them through this dealer for seven or eight times as much as I got. They were both making a fortune off me, only I didn't know it. It never occurred to me at that time that my work could sell for that much."

"Didn't you suspect something when you never saw the work displayed in her home?"

"I never saw her home."

"I don't understand how you could have loved her

and . . . Oh, I guess I'm a little slow on the uptake. She was married?"

He nodded. "Her husband was a wealthy clothing manufacturer, but he was very tightfisted with her allowance. She saw my paintings as a way to make some money on the side without his knowing it. I should have realized that if she would betray her husband with me, she would betray me just as easily. But one good thing came out of it. My name finally became established, and I learned the strange phenomenon that if you ask a hundred or two hundred dollars, nobody thinks it's a work of art. At twenty thousand it's a masterpiece."

"Not so strange," Raine mused. "I remember one of our customers had an old refrigerator she wanted to get rid of. It still worked fine, so she put an ad in the paper, offering it free to anyone who wanted to come and take if off her hands. Nobody called. So my dad told her to advertise it for fifty dollars. She did and got hundreds of calls."

"It's the same with people," he said, running his hand lazily over the length of her body. "You also have to put a high value on yourself, not give your love away too cheaply or for the wrong reasons. If you are too open and trusting, people will use you for their own ends, whether it's to perpetuate a fantasy or make a profit. And finding out you've been used is the worst kind of betrayal."

Her stomach did a flip-flop. If only he knew what she had been using him for. "But in a way I'm using you as the inspiration for my poetry," she said carefully.

He chuckled and hugged her to him. "You don't use someone for inspiration. It would be like using moonlight for inspiration."

"Or summer rain," she said softly.

He propped himself up on his elbow and looked at her a long moment. "Yes, summer rain."

He kissed her lightly, then as she responded, deepened it.

As she drifted into the euphoria of his caresses, she realized that she could never make her confession now about *Buyer Beware* and still have Ari. No, it was best to go with her first plan. She would simply quit the magazine quietly and never tell him.

There was no reason he ever had to know. Weren't there women who still pretended to be virgins on their wedding nights? This would simply remain one of those dark little secrets he'd never find out about.

And he probably wouldn't have if Nicole Prasteau hadn't walked into the gallery on Monday morning.

## CHAPTER TWELVE

Raine left Ari's house early in the morning and returned to her apartment to shower, then met him back in Beverly Hills. When she walked into the gallery it was as if she had entered a magic castle. Her own effervescence was reflected in the crystal paintings, and her love for Ari was reflected back at her in his eyes.

They held each other for a long, languid moment, and he said, "I haven't seen you for an hour and it seems like an eternity."

"I had to go home to change."

"A waste of time this driving back out to Burbank every time you need to change your clothes. Why don't you pack them all up and hang them in my closet?"

Raine's eyes widened. "Move in with you?"

"It's more sensible, isn't it?"

"Are you sure you want to see that much of me? At work *and* at home?"

"Even that wouldn't be enough."

Her hopelessly bourgeois mind immediately made the quantum leap to wondering if this was the first step toward marriage. Then she reminded herself that she'd really only known him a few weeks. Hardly enough to base the decision of a lifetime on.

"I've never lived with a man before," she said uneasily.

"There's nothing to it. I won't be one of those chauvinists who expect a woman to cook and do all the housework."

"You won't chain me to a hot stove?"

"Never."

"And you'll share the vacuuming and the laundry?"

"No. I have a maid who comes twice a week, and if neither of us feels like cooking we'll eat out."

She lifted her chin. "I insist on paying rent."

"Don't be silly."

"You have a mortgage payment, don't you?"

"Well, yes, but . . ."

"Whatever your mortgage payment is, we'll simply split it down the middle."

"That's ridiculous. It's probably three times what you're paying in Burbank. I don't want you to pay me anything."

"I'll pay you exactly what I'm paying in rent now, how's that?"

He took her by the shoulders. "Never in my life have I met a woman with so much pride!"

"Ari, I don't want to feel like a . . . a kept woman."

"If we were married, would you feel like a kept woman?"

She broke away from him and sat down at the small desk at the front of the gallery. "I don't want you to think I'm pressuring you into marriage, Ari. We haven't known each other very long and—"

"Long enough. I would marry you in a minute, except that . . ."

He turned away from her and walked across the room.

"Except what?" she pressed him.

"I have the feeling you're keeping something from me. Sometimes I see it in your eyes, as though you wanted badly to tell me, but you're afraid. Last night just before we made love again, it was there."

She'd have to tell him about *Buyer Beware* now, or the secret would always be hanging over them like a dark cloud. If she ever wanted to marry him, she'd have to take the chance. "Ari . . . there is something . . ."

He came toward her. "Tell me, Raine. There can't be any secrets between us."

She felt a tingle race through her. No matter how liberated you were, a proposal from the man you loved tinted the whole universe a rosy shade of pink.

She began imagining herself at the altar in a white, well maybe off-white, dress, with Ari looking very dashing at her side as they exchanged vows. It was a beautiful image—one that disintegrated the minute Nicole Prasteau walked in.

Raine's heart stopped. She hoped the woman wouldn't see her, but with only two people in the gallery it was inevitable. Then she hoped that Nicole wouldn't recognize her.

Why hadn't it occurred to her that some of those gallery owners she'd spoken to might eventually show up? And Nicole Prasteau, who seemed to be the only one in Los Angeles to carry Ari's work, had to have a close association with him.

"Ari, my darling," Nicole said as she swept into the gallery. Raine felt no pang of jealousy at the "my darling." For all the warmth it denoted, she could have been saying, "Ari, my refrigerator."

The feelings seemed to be mutual. "Nicole," he said coolly.

At that moment she spied Raine, who was making the startling discovery that there was no place to hide in an art gallery. Why hadn't she fallen in love with a sculptor who worked in bronze or marble, she thought frantically.

Ari made the introduction. "Nicole Prasteau, allow me to introduce Raine Walken. She's my new"—he smiled as he thought of an appropriate term—"my new associate."

"Oh, so she's working for you," said Nicole, hanging icicles on every word. "I might have figured you'd do something underhanded to undermine me."

Raine could feel the embarrassment creep up her skin like flames burning her at the stake.

Ari looked from her to Nicole. "What are you talking about?"

Nicole gave a derisive laugh. "I suppose now you're going to pretend you don't know. You thought maybe I wouldn't remember her face? Hah! I remember it very well."

"When did you meet Nicole?" His voice was low, but he was looking at Raine with suspicion. Once again she considered running out of the gallery. She wished now that she'd had the nerve to tell him the truth days, even minutes, ago. This was the worst possible way for him to learn.

"I love how you play the innocent," scoffed Nicole. "Your associate, or whatever you call her, probably really your latest mistress, came into my gallery a few weeks ago. At first she pretended she was interested in buying one of your lithographs, then she came up with a story about how she was doing an article on art gallery rip-offs for some magazine. But now I see what she was really doing. She was your spy. You sent her down to my gallery to see what I was charging for your work. That was a very underhanded, sneaky thing to do."

"And you're an expert in those matters," said Ari.

Then he turned on Raine, a look of disbelief on his face. "So there really was an article."

"I tried to tell you," she said weakly.

"Apparently, not hard enough."

"Don't you remember that night in Malibu I told you I was a consumer reporter, and you didn't believe me."

"You told me it was some ridiculous story about how the Beverly Hills rich squandered their money."

"As in the purchase of overpriced art," she said in a weak voice.

"Which you were so enthusiastically selling." He was beginning to seethe with fury. "So you were working for me *and* the magazine at the same time? Pocketing a few commissions while you picked up information to rake me over the coals. Nice work, Raine."

"I was going to give you back the commissions and salary when I told you."

"And when was that?"

"Last week, but then I decided to quit the magazine when . . ." She gestured helplessly.

"But you haven't yet," he said.

"Well, I haven't called them yet, no. But I was going to today."

She could see the color mounting in his face and a surprised, slightly amused expression on Nicole Prasteau's patrician features.

He couldn't believe he had been so taken in. He had vowed he'd never do it again, and he had been led like a lamb to the slaughter by a pair of sultry green eyes. Why hadn't he listened to his gut feelings? "Get out," he said softly to Raine.

She stood up and went over to him. "Ari, please let me explain."

He turned away from her as though she were poison.

"Ari, I . . ."

"Get out," he said again, and this time with so much vehemence that she didn't dare disobey. She'd come back another time when he had cooled down and make him understand. She had to.

Desperately needing advice, she called the *Buyer Beware* office and asked for Janet.

"Where are you?" her sister asked.

"Beverly Hills. Can we meet someplace? I've got to talk to you."

"Come on down here and we'll go next door to Patty's."

"Can we meet somewhere else? I don't want McCracken or Mrs. Grasset to see me."

"Why not?"

"Because they might ask questions and I'll start to cry."

"You sound like you're crying right now."

"I am."

"Good Heavens, Raine. Look, why don't I meet you at the Egg and I on Wilshire. We'll have an omelette and a glass of wine and you'll feel better."

Since Raine could barely see the street through her tears, the Egg and I made sense. She had only to point her car east on Wilshire and concentrate on the stop lights. But it was an unfortunate choice in that the restaurant was directly across from the Los Angeles County Art Museum, which reminded her of Ari and what a mess she was in.

Janet was already there and greeted her sister worriedly. "You look awful."

"Thanks."

"Don't mention it. What happened?"

"Ari," she said, stifling back a sob. "He wanted to marry me."

"Marriage? I take back everything I've ever said about flaky artistic types who never want to make commitments. Maybe he's not so bad after all. That is," she added skeptically, "if it's not just a line."

With that, Raine let loose such a torrent of tears that Janet had to ask the bartender for a paper napkin.

"It's so embarrassing to cry in public," she sniffed.

"Don't be silly, Raine. People do it all the time. If you can laugh in public, you certainly can cry in public. Now, tell me about Ari. You were so crazy about him. Why are you upset because he wants to marry you? Do you think he was just handing you a line?"

"No, he meant it. The problem was he found out about *Buyer Beware.*"

"I thought you were going to tell him about that." Janet signaled the waitress that they were ready for a table.

"I never quite got around to it," she explained. "You see, he started telling me about these horrible women who had used him, and I couldn't bring myself to admit I was one of that ilk."

"So how did he find out?"

"One of the gallery owners I'd interviewed for the article walked in. Do you remember the one I told you about who had his litho for half price? She thought I was a spy for Ari."

"A *spy!* What is this, East Berlin? These art gallery owners operate like the KGB! Oh, Rainey, all this stuff about spies and price gouging and ghouls lurking around waiting for artists to die. It's all so sordid."

"But Ari isn't like that."

"I know you're in love with him, but don't forget he was jacking up his prices not by just a few hundred dollars, but by several thousand. Honey, dry your eyes. Enough tears over this creep." She took Raine's hand. "I knew I should have made a better case against him from the start. Then you wouldn't have gotten all involved with him. Oh, Rainey, I hate to see you like this."

"Janet, there isn't anything you could have said or done."

"That night you saw him in Malibu. I could have—"

"There's no sense mulling over what might have been," she said with a heavy sigh.

"You're absolutely right. You've just got to put him behind you now. Things always turn out for the best."

"Janet, this was the *worst!* I hate when you start reciting those cheerleader platitudes."

"That's exactly what you need right now. You've got to think positive." Raine groaned, but Janet ignored her and plunged on. "Remember, you still have your job at *Buyer Beware*. Finish up that article and go on to the next one. McCracken wants us to start ordering those long-distance services for a survey on prices and service. We'll be able to call Mom a couple times a week and all our old friends in Chicago. Think of what fun that'll be."

The waitress showed them to their table, but Raine put down the menu. Food was the last thing on her mind. "I'll have to tell McCracken I can't do the article on art galleries," she said.

"Why on earth not?"

Raine shook her head and dabbed her eyes. "It wouldn't be right."

"Would Woodward or Bernstein have refused to expose Watergate if he'd fallen in love with Tricia Nixon? Of course not. Put this crazy idea out of your head. Besides, McCracken is not going to take kindly to putting you on a story for two weeks and having you suddenly decide you can't do it because you fell in love with the subject. He'd fire you so fast your head would spin." Seeing the abject look on her sister's puffy face, Janet softened her tone. "I'd love to have you move back in with me and you know you're always welcome, but you wanted your independence and sometimes that involves making harsh decisions. What are you going to do when your rent comes due next week?"

Since Raine was ignoring the menu, Janet took it upon herself to order them two guacamole omelettes and another glass of chilled zinfandel.

Raine only pushed her food around on her plate and sipped disconsolately at the wine. As always, her sister was dead right when it came to practical matters. She had no choice but to go back to *Buyer Beware* and finish the article.

Back at the office Raine tried to put her notes in order and even managed a paragraph or two on the startling prices of coffee makers on Rodeo Drive. But her heart wasn't in it. She had to talk to Ari.

Taking a deep breath, she dialed his number.

"Ari, can we get together?"

"No." His voice was cold, matter-of-fact.

"Please . . ."

"No, Raine. It's over between us."

"To hell it is!" she yelled as she slammed the phone down. Several writers looked up from their typewriters.

McCracken stubbed out a cigarette and came over to her desk. "Walken, I know how involved you get in a story, but you can't let it get to you."

"I'm afraid I'm in this one way over my head," she said, her fingers still shaking on the receiver.

Grabbing her purse, she ran out the door. She was

in love with Ari Lekas, and she wasn't going to let him go without a fight, or at least an explanation. If he wanted to throw her out of his gallery, he'd have to do it bodily.

## CHAPTER THIRTEEN

Raine parked her car and stormed up Rodeo Drive with all the grim determination of a Green Beret on a life-and-death mission. Well, that's exactly what this is, she thought, as she swung her shoulder bag behind her and turned the corner at Brighton Way.

If nothing else, she would make Ari sit down and listen to her story from beginning to end. He'd have to hear her out and know how much she loved him. Why, he'd . . .

The sight of the gallery temporarily made her lose her train of thought. She stopped, squared her shoulders, and reached in her purse and pulled out a lipstick, reapplying some color to the bottom lip. She had nervously bitten her lips so much that she had eaten off all the lipstick.

Perhaps a Green Beret wasn't an appropriate image. A Canadian Mountie was far more appropriate. "We always get our man," she muttered under her breath, and gave the plate-glass door a push.

But it didn't budge. Then she saw the sign. Closed.

How could he do this to me, she silently raged. Then she glanced sheepishly at her watch. It was after six. Okay, so Green Berets and Canadian Mounties didn't overlook details like this. But of course they didn't have details like lipstick to remember either.

Dejectedly she let out her breath. Where would he

be? Sipping champagne and nibbling caviar? How dare he! The thought was so appalling that she quickly dismissed it. No, he must be suffering in silence somewhere. Home, probably.

Raine hesitated a moment. Should she go up to his house in Laurel Canyon? Wasn't that rather forward?

No more forward than accosting him in his gallery, she answered herself. And in a suddenly imagined scenario, she pictured them making up among the glittering paintings in his living room. With all the memories assaulting him, how could he resist her? Bolstered up by this thought, she quickened her pace as she walked back down Rodeo Drive to her car.

Driving up Sunset Boulevard, she was almost happy picturing how he would greet her at the front door. Of course he'd be angry at first, but after she'd had a chance to talk to him, he would take her in his arms and tell her he still wanted her to move in. No, he would settle for nothing less than marriage and insist they fly to Las Vegas that very night. Maybe they would honeymoon in the Greek islands. She was already planning to listen to Berlitz cassettes so she could speak to his family. His mother, at least, being Canadian born, would understand her. Unless she was French Canadian. Well, that was easy enough. She already owned some French Berlitz cassettes.

The traffic on Laurel Canyon was heavy owing to commuters going over the hill into the San Fernando Valley. She tapped the steering wheel impatiently and was grateful when she finally got up to the signal and could make her left turn on Lookout Mountain Drive, then head up Wonderland.

Thinking of Ari and their honeymoon, she nearly drove right by his house. It was dark and there was no sign anywhere of his Italian sports car. But who'd leave an expensive car like that parked on the street?

There didn't appear to be any lights on, but that could just mean he was in the back.

Turning off the ignition, she walked up the stairs to the front door. Although her knees were giving way under her, she couldn't back down now.

She rang the doorbell and waited. A dog next door barked, but she couldn't detect any noise inside the house. She rang again. No answer.

The bastard, she muttered. He probably was out somewhere sipping champagne! A burning rage consumed her as she returned to her car.

What now?

Wait here? At four A.M. he would arrive home and see her asleep at the wheel, and be so moved by her devotion that he would carry her into his house and . . .

No, Raine, you're not that much of a martyr to sit in a car outside his house all night. It was cramped and uncomfortable, and by the time he got home she'd probably look a wreck. Besides, the neighbor watering his lawn across the street was already eyeing her suspiciously. He probably thought she was casing his place for a robbery.

The most sensible thing was to go home and take Janet's advice, forget all about him. But what she'd actually do is sit in the Jacuzzi for an hour and stew. At any rate, she couldn't chase all over town trying to find him.

Feeling deflated, she drove down Wonderland, still hoping any minute she'd see the black sports car whizzing by her. At the corner of Lookout Mountain and Laurel she debated whether to turn left and return to Burbank, or right and go back into Beverly Hills.

It wouldn't hurt just to stop at the caviar restaurant and see if he was there. He might be sitting at the bar alone mulling over his mistake in letting her go. She would walk up and sit down quietly next to him. He'd look up and, turning those midnight eyes on her, flash her a grateful smile. "I'm glad you came back," he'd say, putting his arms around her. "I love you, Raine. I can't live without you."

She sighed, and resuming her fantasy of a Greek island cruise, she turned right.

As she walked into the restaurant, two men in business suits looked her up and down discreetly and she pretended not to notice. The bar area was dark, but a quick survey told her Ari wasn't sitting there morosely stuffing himself with caviar.

Trying not to look like a call girl drumming up business, she plunged farther back to the booths, passing several with men and women sitting close, gazing into each other's eyes, but no Ari Lekas.

Then suddenly she caught sight of the back of a golden head of hair with a very feminine hand running her manicured fingers through it. He turned slightly and she recognized the grin. The *grin?*

Her heart was pounding to the rhythm of jungle drums. It was the one scenario she had not allowed herself. He was actually out on the town with another woman.

Searing rage swept like flames over her, burning the picture of him and that woman into her mind. All logical, rational thought ceased. A voice told her to turn and run, but her legs were propelling her toward his table.

The woman sitting beside him saw her first. "There is a woman coming over here, Ari, who looks as though if she had a gun she might kill you."

Ari looked up. He had seen Raine in many different lights, but never so beautiful and terrifying and passionate. Never had a woman aroused such a sense of awe in him. His whole body was electrified. He couldn't take his eyes off her. No wonder he had fallen in love with her.

But it was like being in love with a Bengal tiger. They were beautiful creatures; you could admire them, even love them passionately, but you did not bring one home to live with you.

"Do you think she's carrying a gun?" asked the woman nervously, removing her caressing hand from Ari's head.

"I don't know."

Raine stood there a moment, feeling foolish and not knowing what to say. "I want to talk to you," she finally blurted out.

He shook his head.

The woman looked at Ari. "Is this your wife or something?"

"No," he said quietly.

"Wonderful," said the woman, taking a gulp of champagne. "Do you even know her?"

"Not very well, I'm afraid."

Raine clenched her teeth and glared at him. "I'll tell you one thing, you'll never forget me, you bastard." Picking up his glass, she flung the champagne in his face, then turning on her heel, she marched out of the restaurant.

Ari watched her walk through the tables. It was all he could do to restrain himself from running after her.

"That was rude," sniffed the woman at his side.

Still watching Raine, he stood up. "Sorry, I've got to be going," he told the woman absently. "It was nice to see you again, uh . . ." What was her name? He couldn't remember.

"Candy," she said, helping him out.

They had met a few months ago at a dinner party given by mutual friends. She had recognized him as he was closing up the gallery and suggested they have a drink together. It had seemed like a good idea at the time. He was still furious about Raine's betrayal and could have used the distraction of an attractive woman. The trouble was, she wasn't distracting enough. Would any woman ever be after Raine Walken? He left some cash on the table to cover the bill.

"Give my regards to Ray and Lily next time you see them," he told Candy, and walked out.

His first and strongest impulse was to drive to Burbank. God, how he wanted her. But he reminded himself again how she'd used him.

He thought back to that night in Malibu. She had told him a semblance of the truth, but it had been couched in so many lies he hadn't believed her, and she had done nothing subsequently to set him straight. No, she had deliberately set about deceiving him, and this business about her meaning to tell him was just another one of her lies . . . like pretending to be in love with him.

He had to wonder what subconscious masochistic tendency made him fall in love with women who were only out to plot his ruin? Not only had Nicole taken his paintings as gifts, then sold them for enormous profits, but now, after all those years of despair when he had finally established a solid reputation, she was discrediting him by taking the few gifts she had left and drastically undercutting his prices in order to establish her own gallery.

But at least with Nicole the motivation was clear. Greed. There was nothing personal in it. Every gallery owner in town who carried contemporary art was ready to strangle her for her attempts to undercut them.

But Raine's treachery was a mystery. He had felt all along she was holding something back, but why this?

Why did she want to do a splashy exposé about Beverly Hills that might sell a few magazines? What was she getting out of it? It couldn't be money. Reporters didn't make that much. She had pocketed more in commissions than she probably made in a month. It galled him to think of the hypocrisy of her taking those checks, then turning around and writing an article criticizing Beverly Hills prices. He remembered the day he'd sent her out for a coffee maker. Was she really that outraged at the price gouging of the rich?

It seemed to him that if one liked causes, there were far more worthy ones. In his experience, hard-nosed crusaders usually committed themselves to campaigns to stop the slaughter of baby seals or Indian elephants. The sad plight of the overcharged Beverly Hills socialite was hardly the stuff that brought tears of sympathy to one's eyes.

Well, at least he could rest easy that if she did her research, he had nothing to fear from an exposé. A little checking with reputable dealers, especially the ones who handled him in New York, and she'd be able to verify the value of his work, despite anything Nicole Prasteau might have said.

Damn, but he'd been naive and trusting. Well, not entirely. There had always been that gut feeling. And yet, he had been so sure she loved him. Why else would she have come storming into the restaurant tonight?

He thought about the past week. Until Raine had joined him, he'd hated working in the gallery. With her jokes and lively conversation, she'd made it seem like fun. His whole life had changed since she entered it. He'd even begun a new painting.

Summer Rain. He felt a tug inside his chest. God help him, but he still wanted her.

No, he told himself sternly. Forget her. You can

never fully domesticate a Bengal tiger. Hadn't he learned his lesson with Nicole? Raine had betrayed him once, she'd do it again.

Raine knew she shouldn't be driving a car in her murderous state, but now all she wanted was to get home and into the bubbling numbness of a Jacuzzi. Whatever betrayal she had wrought by not telling him about *Buyer Beware* was minuscule in comparison to his crimes, the least of which, in her mind, was overcharging his customers.

All his talk about wanting to marry her and taking her to meet his family had been empty lies. He had cheapened everything beautiful they'd ever had by turning around and cuddling up to another woman before he'd even given their affair a decent burial.

At least now she'd have no more compunctions about writing that article and showing him up for the unscrupulous liar that he was.

For the next week she committed herself to the article with a fury. What she didn't finish at the office she took home with her and typed till three or four in the morning.

It occurred to her that she could check his prices with galleries in New York, but the article only dealt with Los Angeles. And the facts were that one could get his work at a price considerably cheaper at another gallery here. He couldn't claim ignorance. That he seemed to know Nicole Prasteau quite well was damning enough. What it came down to was that he was deliberately overcharging, and he should be exposed for it.

Janet showed up at her apartment one day after work. "Hi. I'm taking you to dinner."

"Not hungry."

"Not anything," said Janet. "Look at you, circles under your eyes. You're wasting away to nothing because you haven't eaten a decent meal in a week. Snap out of it, Raine. You're going to kill yourself."

"Look," she bristled. "Don't come over here and lecture me, I'm—"

Janet looked at her sister and softened. "Yeah, I know. You're hurting."

"As soon as I finish this article I'll calm down. I just have to get it out of my system."

Janet read over some of what she'd done. "Talk about burning your bridges behind you," she said. "If he reads this, you can forget about a reconciliation."

"Reconciliation is the last thing I want," Raine answered sharply. "And I'd love nothing better than to have him read this. But I doubt if he ever picks up a copy of *Buyer Beware* anyway."

Shuffling through her papers, Janet spied some sheets of poetry. "Hey, these are new. You've really been busy."

"Inspired. Read them and tell me what you think."

Janet plopped herself down in an armchair and quietly read all of them. "This is the best stuff you've ever done. In fact, from what I've read of your article, I'd say it's the best writing you've done. I'll tell you, Raine, love may not be good for your health, but it's doing wonders for your creativity."

"To hell with my creativity. I just want to forget about Ari. If I could only sleep one night straight through without waking up and thinking about him . . . and that woman. There are times I find myself sitting here like a zombie just staring at the phone hoping he'll call."

"I thought you said you weren't interested in a reconciliation."

"I'm not. I just want him to call so I can tell him to

go to hell." She sighed. "Oh, Janet, it wasn't this bad when the guitarist left me."

"You just don't remember. You were plenty heartbroken then too, and you got over it."

"But I wasn't angry then, just hurt. It's the fury that eats up your insides."

"Anger doesn't last and wounds heal. But not if you don't get some nourishment into your system. How about enchiladas down at that Mexican place you love. You know, the one with the mariachis? We'll have strawberry margaritas and—"

She groaned. "Any place but there."

Raine gradually regained her appetite, but the memories of Ari didn't recede. When her article came out it was almost a relief. It meant she was finally finished with the subject.

That night she was sitting at home alone watching the six o'clock news on television when suddenly she was shocked to see Pauline Millian, the station's consumer reporter, holding up a copy of *Buyer Beware* and talking about Beverly Hills art galleries.

Before Raine could dial Janet's number, they were showing an interview with Ari inside his gallery. He was angrily denying that he overcharged for his work and was saying that he had hired a lawyer and was going to sue *Buyer Beware*.

Raine blinked several times, hoping what she was seeing was some aberrant nightmare fantasy.

The telephone rang and she jumped. It was Janet. "Did you just see that piece on the news?"

"Yes," she said weakly.

"Ari looked fit to be tied."

"He has a way of looking like that when he's mad." Just then the doorbell rang. "Hang on a minute, somebody's at the door."

"Don't just answer it," warned Janet. "First ask who it is."

"Who is it?" Raine called out.

"Ari."

## CHAPTER FOURTEEN

For a moment Raine hesitated to open the door. Was he violent enough to rip her to shreds? Since he had hired a lawyer, it seemed unlikely. The lawyer would do the ripping. Legally.

"Hello, Ari," she said in a shaky voice. He was wearing tan slacks and a forest-green polo shirt, looking even more marvelous than she remembered, with his ragged blond hair and dark eyes. If only he didn't have such a scowl on his face.

He stood there for a moment glaring at her, then handed her the latest copy of *Buyer Beware*. "What the hell were you trying to do to me?"

"I was just—"

He brushed past her and walked into the apartment. "Damn it, Raine. You had no right to make these kinds of accusations!"

"Ari, I was only going on—"

"What? Did you check with any of the other galleries that carried my work besides Nicole Prasteau's?"

"I couldn't find any others in Los Angeles and—"

"Because there weren't any," he snapped.

"Would you let me finish a sentence?"

He sat down on her daybed. "Go ahead. Finish. I want to hear what you have to say."

She had never seen him in such a rage, not even the

day he found out she was working for *Buyer Beware*. Though she was sure he wouldn't hit her, he was nonetheless a little terrifying.

Moving away from him, she leaned against the kitchen counter to keep her balance. "When I went into Nicole Prasteau's gallery, I pretended to be a customer, and she told me her prices were quite a bit lower than yours. She even told me that she could get me the ten-thousand-dollar litho I loved for five thousand."

"Of course she could. I gave it to her."

Raine blinked her eyes. "Why would you just give your work away to another gallery?"

"It was before she had a gallery, and I gave them to her because I was in love with her."

Raine stared at him uncomprehendingly for a few seconds. Then suddenly she realized what had happened. "She was the married woman in New York you told me about?" Raine threw back her head and shut her eyes. "Why, that—"

"Be careful whom you call what. I'd like to know why you didn't mention what she'd said to me."

"Because . . . well, I just assumed she was telling the truth. What am I supposed to think when she's charging half of what you are? That's not like a ten-percent cash discount or something!"

"It certainly didn't bother *you* to sell my work when you thought it was so overpriced."

"I sent you back those commission checks."

"I'm surprised you didn't send them directly to the customers," he shot back sarcastically. "If you had been up front and asked me for the names of the New York galleries I've authorized to carry my work, they would have confirmed what my paintings are worth on the current market."

"Then why wasn't Nicole charging those prices if she could charge more?" Raine asked suspiciously.

"Nicole had just gotten a divorce, and in her settlement she had come away with close to a million dollars, worth of modern art. Her plan was to undercut everybody, including me, to get her new gallery established here."

"You're a fine one to spew out all the moral indignation. That night in Malibu you told me you were the only one in L.A. who carried your work. You must have known about her gallery and what she was charging," she said accusingly. "Why didn't you tell me then?"

Ari's expression darkened and he looked away from her. "All right. I did know. I'll admit it. It galled me that after everything else she'd pulled on me she would do this too. I knew she only had a few pieces left and after that it would be finished. Do you think I was crazy enough to tell people some of my best work was available for so much less?"

"You could have told me. I think it's hypocritical to be angry at me for keeping something from you when you were doing the same. And what about this business of telling your customers they could double back their investment with your lithographs?" she continued, on the offensive.

"That is absolutely true. And it is something else my dealers in New York could have verified. In the last few years every time one of them has sold, the next one in that edition has gone for twice as much."

"I assumed that was just another sales pitch," she said weakly, and feeling her legs give way, she took a chair opposite Ari.

"You assumed quite a bit."

"I guess I did. Tell me, how in the world did that TV consumer reporter get hold of the story?"

"Pauline Millian is one of my customers. She owns two of my paintings. And she was damn upset about what she read. She called me up to check it out and was so outraged by the lies in your article and by what Nicole was trying to do that she brought her camera crew out to give me an equal chance to reply."

"A little self-interest there too, I imagine. She was afraid the value of her paintings would drop." Raine sighed heavily. "I'm sorry about all this, Ari. I'm sure *Buyer Beware* will print an apology. Are you really going to sue?"

"My attorney is on it. Something like this can seriously damage my reputation and my business. Hell, it can put me out of business. I can't let it slide by." He stood and walked to the door.

She rushed to him and grabbed his arm. "Ari, please . . ."

Her touch burned into his skin. No woman had ever aroused in him such raging feelings, and he hated himself for coming over tonight. He'd thought of little else but Raine these past painful weeks, and now seeing her, having her so close, gazing down at her, he wanted desperately to hold her in his arms. She looked so pale and vulnerable. Tears filled her large green eyes. Unable to fight it anymore, he took her face in his hands and lowered his lips to hers. Damn, but it felt so right, so good, to kiss her.

Then it came back to him in a flood what she had done. What was he getting himself into? She had hurt him once. She would do it again. He couldn't let it happen.

"I was going to tell you about the magazine," she said desperately as he pulled away from her. "You see, I'd planned to quit because I was in love with you and—"

"But you didn't quit."

"Janet talked me into holding out for a week."

"So now you're blaming it on your sister? Raine, when are you going to take responsibility for your own actions?"

"What Janet said made a lot of sense. She didn't want me to quit one job without being sure of another. She was just trying to make sure I didn't do anything rash."

"Deceiving me wasn't rash?"

"She thought I should tell you about *Buyer Beware,* so that was my fault too. I really did think you were overcharging. What else could I think after what Nicole said?"

"But you were still ready to move in with me, thief that I was."

"Because I loved you," she moaned.

"So much that you wrote an article that could destroy my business."

"I wasn't going to write it, but then that night I saw you with that girl, I was so furious I couldn't see straight."

"This," he said angrily, "was all the result of a vendetta?"

"Ari, please, I'm so sorry about all this. Can't you just accept my apology and forget about it?"

"First you come to work for me under false pretenses, then you set about ruining my reputation and my business. And now you want me to overlook everything and forgive you? It's too late for apologies, Raine." Without turning back, he walked out the door.

In tears, she started to call Janet, then put the receiver back. She had wanted her independence. Now she couldn't run crying back to her every time she had a crisis. Ari was right. It was time to take full responsibility for her own actions.

The following morning she could sense the tension at the *Buyer Beware* office when she walked in. All typewriters stopped and there was an eerie silence. Janet rushed up to her. "You didn't call back last night. Is everything okay?"

She nodded. "What's going on here? Why's everyone looking at me as if I just brought in the bubonic plague?"

Janet took her aside. "Mrs. Grasset and McCracken are in a meeting with Lekas's lawyer. Everyone looked pretty grim. Do you think he's really going to sue?"

"I think so. He said that the article could ruin his reputation and his business. And he's right."

The door to Mrs. Grasset's office opened. McCracken and the attorney came out. All typewriters immediately started humming again as McCracken came over to her. "Mrs. Grasset wants to see you in her office."

Raine's heart was pounding as she steeled herself for the inevitable. She was certain she'd be fired.

Mrs. Grasset was sitting behind her desk looking over some papers. "Come on in, Raine, and close the door behind you."

"Mrs. Grasset, I'm terribly sorry about all this."

"Have a seat."

"Thank you."

The tiny woman frowned and tapped her pen on her desk. "It pains me to have to tell you this, Raine. You've been a superb employee and an excellent journalist. Unfortunately, on this particular article, it seems that you did not check your sources very well. And I think you may have let some personal feelings influence what you wrote."

"Yes, I know," she said softly. Raine was wishing that if Mrs. Grasset were going to fire her, she'd be quick about it. The last thing she needed to hear was more lecturing on the subject.

"It looks as if we may be going into some litigation on this matter, and I think it best while this is going on that you go on suspension. That doesn't mean you're fired, of course."

"But it's a suspension without pay, right?"

"That is correct," said Mrs. Grasset. "I've informed accounting, and they'll have your check ready if you want to pick it up tomorrow."

Had Ari really wanted to get back at her so much he'd had his lawyer demand she be suspended? She supposed there was justice in it, but she was still hurt that he would go so far.

Feeling numb, Raine managed to say good-bye to everyone. McCracken felt especially bad. "Hey, let's hope this thing gets resolved fast so I can get you back here. As far as I'm concerned, you wrote what you did on good faith. I've seen reporters make a lot bigger blunders."

Janet started to walk out with her, but Raine stopped her. "I'll be all right."

"Maybe you should move back in with me for the time being."

"No thanks, Janet. I'll manage. If I have to, I'll get another job."

"If you need any money . . ."

"Don't worry. I don't have that much pride. If I find myself out in the street, I'll come banging on your door."

Raine went home and did what thousands of other Southern Californians did when they found themselves out of work. She put on a bathing suit, sat by the pool, read want ads, and tried to keep from crying.

It wasn't as if she couldn't do anything. If worse came to worst, she could always go back to selling appliances. She could forget about applying to newspapers and magazines. Nobody would hire a sloppy journalist who got her company embroiled in lawsuits. But perhaps there was an ad agency copywriting job. Wax eloquent about breakfast cereals and laundry detergent? She shuddered. Well, why not? At least it would be using words creatively.

Starting that afternoon and for the next week, she called every ad agency in town. A few even had her come in for interviews, but nobody had any positions open. Her bank account would hold out one more week. After that she'd look for a sales job. Appliances, clothes, or anything else to stay alive. In the meantime she kept an eye on the want ads and wrote poems feverishly into the night.

More than any other time in her life, the poems were flowing out of her in great gusts like her tears. It was only through her poetry that she could find an outlet for the raging emotions that were consuming her.

She wrote about all the beautiful and poignant moments she'd spent with Ari, about how his paintings made her feel, and about what it had felt like to make love to him and to see him smile at her in the morning.

She tried to imagine what it would have been like without the complications. They'd had so much. It could have been an ideal life with his artwork inspiring her poems and vice versa.

But then, ultimately, she had to write about her role in ruining her relationship with Ari. It had ended only because of her own cowardice. Had she told him the truth, they might still be together.

She had wanted to keep these feelings to herself, but it was too much to keep bottled up, and finally she asked her sister to read what she'd written. Janet started to cry when she put them down. "This is the most beautiful work you've ever done, Raine."

"You do think so?"

She nodded. "I guess I didn't understand before. You're really in love with that guy, aren't you?"

Raine sighed. "I must be. At least doing the poetry keeps me from going crazy thinking about him."

Janet ran her fingers through her short-cropped hair. "I feel so guilty, Raine."

"Why in the world should you feel guilty?"

"Because I was the one who talked you into going ahead with the article. I should have made you check out more sources. I should have insisted you tell him the truth. I should have—"

"Janet, it's not your fault. I appreciate your wanting to lift the responsibility from my shoulders, but whatever mess I've gotten myself into, it's my own fault. You were the one who told me I should tell him the truth and I didn't."

Janet put her arm around Raine's shoulder. "Well, whatever else has come out of this, the poetry is wonderful. You've got to try and publish this. It's too good to keep hidden away."

Raine shook her head. "It's too personal. You're moved by it because you know me. Nobody else would care."

"Will you let me make some copies to send to some small local publishers at least?"

"Go ahead, but I think it's a waste of time."

Janet made copies the next day, sending them to three publishers with short cover letters. Then, even though she knew Raine wouldn't like it, and she didn't dare tell her, she sent copies of the poems with a personal note to Ari Lekas.

## CHAPTER FIFTEEN

Within a week one of the poetry submissions was returned with a kind, personally written rejection letter. The editor had loved the poems, but unfortunately they had discontinued publishing poetry since there was no longer a market for it. Not unexpected news, but depressing nonetheless.

Raine had just finished her fifth nonproductive phone call of the morning looking for work as a writer. And just to lighten what was turning out to be another dismal day, she'd even called Disney studios and demanded to know what Geppetto had against marriage.

When the phone rang, she jumped on it, muttering, "Please let it be someone offering me a job."

"Hey, Walken. McCracken here. You're the hardest person to get ahold of. That line's been busy all morning. You running a mail-order operation out of your apartment now?"

She laughed. It was good to hear that familiar gravelly voice. "How are you, McCracken? What's going on?"

"Same old thing. Just wanted to tell you Lekas withdrew his suit and Grasset wants you to come back."

"You're kidding."

"Would I kid about something like that? No, I'm

serious. Your sister told me you were job hunting, and I wanted to catch you before you took anything. I'd hate to lose you."

She knew she should probably make him think she had some hot prospects, but she was too anxious to go back to work to play that game. "When can I start?"

"Come on in today. I've got a story I want to put you on. You know all those TV ads for alcoholic rehabilitation centers? Well, we're going to check them out, see just what you get for your money."

Her excitement at going back to work paled. "I suppose you'll want me to pretend I'm an alcoholic."

"Yeah. I'd like to do this from the inside if I can, and Grasset's willing to put up the money to get you in some of the places. Should be a hell of a story."

"I'm sure it will be," she said, trying to inject some enthusiasm into her voice. "Look, I'll get showered and come on in." This was no time to be choosy about work. After all, she'd had too much to drink one night and knew what it felt like to wake up the next morning wishing you'd stayed sober. She got dressed in a hurry and drove to the office.

In spite of her misgivings about going back to consumer reporting, she was glad to see her coworkers. They'd even gone to the trouble of putting up a makeshift banner that read, Welcome Back Raine.

McCracken, the perennial tightwad, even treated her to a stale doughnut from the vending machine. "Good to have you back, Walken," he said with a smile.

"By the way, how come Lekas dropped the lawsuit?" she asked.

"His lawyer didn't say, but I've got a friend who's a close friend of that TV consumer reporter who did the story. I think what happened was that our exposé and the TV coverage had the complete opposite effect of what he expected. People have been grabbing up those paintings like hotcakes."

"They have?" she said with surprise.

He chuckled. "Seems a lot of 'em were ladies who saw him on television and were intrigued to see him in person."

"Figures," she muttered.

"But also a whole flock of wealthy Beverly Hills art collectors descended on him. I guess, before, his work was only known by a kind of elite, but now that everyone knows what an Aristotle Lekas painting costs, everyone wants to have one."

"Will wonders never cease," she mused.

"Yeah, it's hard for a consumer reporter to understand, because we've got the kind of readers who'd drive ten miles out of their way to get a stick of butter that's two cents less than the local supermarket charges. Beverly Hills is a whole different ball game. It's like if you drive a Rolls-Royce, right away everyone knows how much it cost, so they're suitably impressed. Now an Aristotle Lekas painting has become like a Rolls-Royce. You walk into somebody's house and you see one of those hanging over the couch and you think, hey, this slob can afford to spend forty thousand dollars on a slab of painted canvas. It's like the psychology behind the craze for designer jeans. I mean, let's face it. Why the hell would somebody want to advertise the name of a company on their rear end? We're talking status seekers and snob appeal."

"And that's why doing a consumer exposé on the rich, in the end, means nothing," she said bitterly. "As far as I'm concerned, this whole thing was a waste of time."

"Not according to Grasset," he said. "Sales that week were up twenty-five percent."

She was glad Ari had profited from her mistake, but

it made her sad to think of all the callous status seekers buying his work. They would display it prominently, but it would never mean anything to them. Thank heaven for public museums where people who loved art could go to enjoy it.

Raine was just starting to sift through the folders of alcoholic rehabilitation centers when Janet rushed up to her desk and whispered, "Interesting tidbit. I just talked to Grasset's secretary. You know why Lekas dropped the lawsuit?"

"I just found out from McCracken. Evidently he's been doing a land-office business because of the article."

Janet shook her head. "That's *not* the reason. He called up here to talk to you and was told you'd been suspended. Evidently that upset him, so he called Grasset personally and said he'd drop the lawsuit if you were hired back."

"Come on, Janet. That's ridiculous. He would have liked nothing better than for me to lose my job over this."

"Maybe you underestimate him."

"I doubt it. You should have seen him that night he left my apartment. Nothing would have made him happier than to see my neck in a noose."

"Raine, why don't you call him?"

"No! Are you crazy? I don't understand why all of a sudden you've become his advocate. You used to warn me against these artistic types. Well, you were absolutely right. The next person I date will be a bookkeeper."

Janet sighed. "Raine, I think I may have been wrong about him."

Raine looked up at her sister with surprise. It wasn't usual to hear her admit to being wrong.

"Well, it's true. I've always tried to look after you

and make you think practically. Think like me, actually. And after reading those poems, I realized that you aren't me. You have a genius that I could never hope to have, and maybe you need someone artistic like Ari Lekas to bring that out." She picked up a brochure on one of the alcoholic clinics. "Doing stories like this is only going to stifle all that creativity until someday you might forget you ever were a poet."

Raine was moved by what her sister said, but firmly convinced she was wrong. The artistic types only brought you heartache. And so what if the heartaches brought poetry out of you. The unhappiness that followed wasn't worth it. She picked up the phone and with a new resolve began making appointments at the alcohol clinics, and wondered why nobody started up treatment centers that unhooked people from love.

Eager to prove herself committed to her new assignment, she stayed at the office until eight, then went home utterly exhausted. At the bottom of the stairs she stopped for a moment. Had she really forgotten to turn off the lights before she left that morning? Janet had pounded that into her over the years so solidly that she flicked those switches almost automatically. But then she had been so anxious to start back to work that she might have forgotten.

Barely in the door, she started to kick off her shoes, then, thinking of Janet's admonishments, thought better of it. From now on she was going to be utterly practical in every aspect of her life. She'd begin immediately by putting her shoes in the closet.

Then she saw Ari sitting on her daybed.

"How did you get in here?" she gasped.

"Your sister gave me a key."

"I'll kill her! She had no right to go meddling in my life. I want you out of—" She suddenly caught sight of the painting propped up on an easel across the room and walked slowly over to it.

"It will look better with the right spotlights focused on it," he said.

She could barely breathe, it was so beautiful. The sketches she'd seen couldn't do it justice. There were hundreds of diagonal slashes like narrow rods filled with rainbows, and at the bottom were thousands of tiny bubbles like sea foam.

"Summer Rain," he said.

"Summer rain on the ocean," she whispered. Coming close to it, she took in every detail. Very subtle, but visible if one looked closely enough, was her face, her red hair blowing in wisps around it. She was too moved to speak and turned to him, brushing the tears from her eyes.

"It's yours."

She wheeled around to him. "You're giving it to me?"

"You inspired it." He came over and took her in his arms. "Raine, I've missed you."

She looked up into his midnight eyes, and all the pain of the last few weeks seemed to melt away. His lips found hers and he hugged her to him so tightly she thought he would crack a rib.

It felt wonderful to be once again encircled by his love, but she was wary. Breaking away from him, she said, "Did you really call Mrs. Grasset and tell her you'd drop the lawsuit if I got my job back?"

"Raine, I never meant for you to lose your job. That was never one of my demands. My attorney didn't tell me anything about it. When I called and they said you were suspended, I was furious that they'd done that to you."

"Why did you call?"

"Janet sent me your poems."

Raine felt a surge of renewed anger. "The unmitigated gall! I never gave her permission to do that."

He pulled her over to the bed, and before she could protest, he was caressing her.

"I'm glad she sent me the poems," he said. "Until then I was still feeling betrayed and used. I wondered if you had ever really loved me. And then I read what you'd written and I knew."

"You should have known that I loved you," she said softly, pressing kisses like gifts onto his face. "When did you finish the painting?"

"After you left I hired someone to work in the gallery so I could concentrate on it. I was burning to get it done, hoping it would help me take my mind off you. But it only made me realize how much I needed you. And then when I read the poems, I knew how necessary you and I both are to each other. You don't know how much I've missed the feel of you in my arms, your smile every morning, the sight of your wonderful red hair, the sound of your laughter. I want you to see the slides Diego took—how well they'll go with your poems. We've got to finish that book, then start on another."

"I don't know about my coming back to work in the gallery," she said hesitantly.

"Neither of us should be working in a retail store," he said quickly. "I've already made arrangements with another gallery in town to take over my work. Merchandising my own work was destroying me. We both need the freedom to create. We need exposure to new places and ideas. We could start on our honeymoon in Europe. I want to read your poems about the Ile St. Louis at dawn, the Acropolis at sunset, and—"

*"Honeymoon?"* she interrupted him.

"If we're getting married, we should have a honeymoon."

"That does seem logical." She looked up at him with wonder. "Though I suppose we could have a honeymoon first and then get married."

He laughed. "We could, I suppose. You and I aren't the most logical people in the world. There's no reason we have to do things as everybody else does, but if it's all the same to you, I'd rather introduce you to my family as my wife."

"Do you suppose our children will be as crazy and impractical as we are?"

"Let's hope they take after their Aunt Janet so they can look after us in our old age."

"Maybe by that time we'll have our heads out of the clouds."

He hugged her tightly. "No, my love, let's hope to God that never happens."